Kabbalah

Kabbalah

A Love Story

RABBI LAWRENCE KUSHNER

MORGAN ROAD BOOKS

New York

MORGAN ROAD BOOKS

KABBALAH: A LOVE STORY. Copyright © 2006 by Lawrence Kushner. All rights reserved. No part of this book may be reproduced or transmitted in any form or by any means, electronic or mechanical, including photocopying, recording, or by any information storage and retrieval system, without written permission from the publisher. Published by Morgan Road Books, an imprint of The Doubleday Broadway Publishing Group, a division of Random House, Inc.

PRINTED IN THE UNITED STATES OF AMERICA

MORGAN ROAD BOOKS and the M colophon are trademarks of Random House, Inc.

This book is a work of fiction. Names, characters, businesses, organizations, places, events, and incidents either are the product of the author's imagination or are used fictitiously. Any resemblance to actual persons, living or dead, events, or locales is entirely coincidental.

Visit our Web site at www.morganroadbooks.com

BOOK DESIGN BY AMANDA DEWEY

CALLIGRAPHY BY CAROLE LOWENSTEIN

Library of Congress Cataloging-in-Publication Data
Kushner, Lawrence, 1943–
Kabbalah : a love story / Lawrence Kushner.
p.   cm.
1. Cabala—Fiction. 2. Judaism—Fiction. 3. Mysticism—Fiction. 4. Spiritual life—Fiction. 5. New York (N.Y.)—Fiction. 6. Jews—New York (State)—Fiction. I. Title.
PS3611.U738K33 2006
813'.6—dc22
2005052091

ISBN-13: 978-0-7679-2412-2
ISBN-10: 0-7679-2412-6

1   3   5   7   9   10   8   6   4   2

FIRST EDITION

for Danny Matt
who first opened the Zohar for me
and for Eddie Feld
who reads it with me

In none of their systems did the kabbalists fail to stress the interrelation of all worlds and levels of being. Everything is connected with everything else, and this interpenetration of all things is governed by exact though unfathomable laws.

◆

—GERSHOM GERHARD SCHOLEM

Time is just God's way of making sure that everything doesn't happen all at once.

◆

—GEORGE CARLIN

Acknowledgments

I am grateful for the advice and teaching of my friends: Martin Cohen, Richard Davis, Ed Feld, Art Green, Josh Holo, Robert Jossen, Danny Matt, Phil Miller, Paul Needham, Jonathan Omer-man, Nehehmia Polen, Lawrence Rudnick, Howard Smith, Laurie Wolf-Polen, and Elliot Wolfson.

Many have also kindly endured earlier drafts of this fable and shared their gentle criticisms: Linda Blackstone, Anita Diamant, Merle Feld, Nancy Gennet, Bernie Horn, David Mamet, Rebecca Pidgeon, Barbara Shuman, Joseph Skibel, Lorel Zar-Kessler, and my five wonderful children, Noa, Michael, Zachary, Madhavi, and Lev. It seems only fitting that I also mention here the perfect coffee brewed by Naser Almualla and Yamen Eltawil at Notes from Underground café on Green and Van Ness, where all the mugs read, "Don't talk to me before I finish this."

I also want to acknowledge the unfailing support of Steve Pearce, senior rabbi, and Gary Cohn, executive director, as well as the officers and members of The Congregation Emanu-El of San Francisco who have invited me to serve as a resident teacher and writer in their community. Without their vision and generosity, I would not have had the time to complete this book.

Four women in both professional and mysterious ways have made this novel a reality: Winnifred Gallagher, a friend and writer about religion, introduced me to Kris Dahl; Kris Dahl, my sage and amazing agent, who said, "I really like this. I want to show it to Phyllis Grann"; Phyllis Grann, my editor, who saw the real story through the original manuscript's underbrush; and finally, Debbie Danielpour Chapel, my fiction teacher extraordinaire without whose encouragement this book surely would never have been written.

But most of all I am aware (again) of the patience, confidence, counsel, and love of my life partner, Karen. Like when we were courting almost forty years ago, still, after all these years: "*Libav-tini b'ahat may-ae-naiykh*—You have stolen my heart with a single glance."

L.K.
San Francisco, 2006

Kabbalah

ONE

MANHATTAN

On this day the light had disguised itself as the first ordinary orange rays of a September sunrise over the East River. It easily eclipsed the big red neon Tower Records sign and silhouetted all the sheets of newspaper scurrying over Broadway's empty sidewalks. It ricocheted off the windows on the building across the street and then flooded Kalman's office. And for a moment, light was everywhere. And everything was light.

Kalman opened the door and squinted in the brightness. Winded from climbing three flights up the utility stairwell, he was proud his forty-six-year-old constitution could still take them in stride. He set his coffee on the desk, hung his parka over the back of a chair, and began unpacking his bag—teaching notes, books, a folder of last week's marked-up homework. Finally, he peeled the tape from the flap of a bubble-wrap envelope protecting a very old volume of Zohar, the master text of Kabbalah. Kalman had picked it up in Israel decades earlier; the caretaker of a little out-of-the-way synagogue had given it to him.

"Here," the old man had said. "Take it, it's yours—has your name on it."

So he took it. He'd been using it ever since as a pedagogic prop, a teaching aid for his courses on mysticism. How could he possibly have imagined that, after all these years, the back cover of the book was about to come unglued and give birth to another page? That's the way it is with a good book: Just when you think you've read all its words, the damn thing falls apart in your hands and you have to start all over again.

The leather of the cover was long gone; only the interior pastedowns had survived the continents and centuries. Similarly, all that remained of the binding was naked stitch work. The back cover was even more distressed—a sandwich of several barely-glued-together and delaminating layers. The extremes of New York's climate had taken their toll on what-ever adhesive properties the old glue might still have pos-sessed. Indeed, the book was so insubstantial, it seemed more pneumatic than corporeal—a child's helium balloon in im-minent danger of floating away. The paper of the pages had a bluish cast and was so softly textured, it felt like cloth; worm-holes embroidered the edges and much of the gutter. Many margins were embellished with handwritten notes. The title page bore the names or biblical verses poetically alluding to the names of generations of owners. And at the bottom there was printed a verse from the Book of Job: "What is hidden shall come into the light."

Then, like a man swearing an oath in court, Kalman placed his open palm on the book and mused, "And what was hidden has come to me!" He closed his eyes and smiled.

Kalman's office was at the back of the library stacks, a destination distinguished primarily by the fact that it could be reached from the stairway door by at least half a dozen different paths. And each one was through a different maze of aisles created by floor-to-ceiling gray metal shelves of books and—if you bothered to flip on the switches as you walked by—illuminated by overhead fluorescent lights. There were routes for every mood: You could walk through medieval Europe and the Holocaust; you could walk through commentaries on the Hebrew Bible, the New Testament, or the Koran; you could walk through the Talmud, the history of Israel, Jewish ethics, or Jewish humor. But no matter which path you chose, it was through books, literally thousands and thousands of them, all waiting patiently for readers like flowers for bees.

"So you're interested in becoming a rabbi. . . ." Kalman set down her letter and smiled at the red-haired young woman sitting on the other side of his desk.

"Yes, I am, Rabbi Stern. I'm particularly interested in Kabbalah."

"Which is why, I suppose, the dean asked *me* to meet with you."

She nodded.

Kalman looked over his reading glasses. "Does God talk to you?"

"Not that I know of."

"Well, that's a good sign."

"I majored in classics and religion at Brown. I even took a year of Hebrew. For the past several years, I have tried Buddhist meditation, spent six months in India on an ashram, and then last year I had an epiphany. I was at my nephew's bar mitzvah, and it dawned on me that Judaism must have something mystical, too."

"Indeed," said Kalman. He reached over, picked up the Zohar, and handed it to her. "Be gentle, it's very, very old."

"When was it published?"

"Look at this line, here," he said, pointing to the verse from Job at the bottom of the title page.

"Why are some of the letters bigger than the others?"

"Gematria."

"You mean where each letter has a numerical equivalent?"

"Excellent." He handed her a pencil and a notepad. "How's your arithmetic?"

"You'll have to help me."

"Let's first wait and see if you need any. . . . Remember, only the *big* letters."

"Okay," she said, "*Ayin* is . . . Wait, don't tell me, *mem, nun, samekh, ayin,* yes, seventy; *lamed* is thirty; *yod* is ten. . . . *Tsadi.* What's *tsadi?*"

"Ninety," said Kalman.

"Thank you. The *aleph,* of course, is one; the *vav* is six; and the *resh* is . . ."

"Two hundred. Relax, this is not a test."

She tallied the numbers and replied with a hesitant grin, "Four hundred and eight?"

"Bingo!" said Kalman, clapping his hands together in mock applause. "Pub date hidden in a scriptural verse."

"But how is four hundred and seven a date?"

"The publisher assumes you know which millennium you're in. So you add the present millennium and get 5407. Then subtract that from the current Hebrew year, 5757, leaving 350. Finally, subtract that from this year, 1997, which tells us the book was published in 1647. Piece of cake. And if that's too complicated for you, just add 240 to the Hebrew year and correct for the proper millennium."

"But I don't understand, Rabbi Stern. Why didn't they just put the date?"

"Because the publisher believed that everything worth knowing is already in the Hebrew Bible. That's what it means to say that God gave it. We only have to learn how to read and interpret those words correctly. That's what we're supposed to be doing here in this school: learning how to read them properly."

SAFED: ITERATION ONE

Kalman watched while the young woman contemplated the book in her hands.

"It's really beautiful, Rabbi Stern. What is it?"

"The red letters at the top of the page."

Falteringly, she sounded out the three words: "*Ha-Zohar al ha-Torah*. The Zohar on the Torah—awesome!" Her cheeks flushed. "I've read about it, but I've never seen one before."

"You are holding the first of a three-volume set that purports to be the transcript of the peripatetic teachings and adventures of the second-century mystic Shimon bar Yohai and his companions as they wander the Galilean hills. Like other rabbinic texts, it humbly claims only to *elaborate* on the real meaning of the Bible. Gershom Scholem . . . you know about him?"

"Historian of mysticism?"

"Yes. Scholem once pointed out that, in a revealed religion like Judaism, creativity must masquerade as commentary."

"I don't understand."

"If everything worth knowing is already in the Torah, then no one can say anything new of any real value. So if you're a Jew and you have a creative idea, you must begin by demonstrating how it's already in scripture."

"And so that's why the Zohar claims to elucidate the Torah?"

"Correct. It was Scholem who also first suggested that the Zohar is a mystical novel. That would make the Zohar a treatise on Kabbalah that has been disguised to *look like* a commentary on the Torah, which, in turn, is masquerading as a novel. Scholars now agree with Scholem that it was pseud-epigraphically written by the Castilian Kabbalist Moshe de Leon toward the end of the thirteenth century."

"It sort of gives ghostwriting a new dimension, doesn't it," she said.

Kalman laughed. "Well, if you believe in the transmigra-tion of souls, I suppose. According to at least one document, Moshe de Leon feared that no one would read something he wrote, so he invented—or I suppose you could say chan-neled—a more prestigious author. But whoever wrote it, the Jews bought the whole thing. After the Hebrew Bible and the Talmud, the Zohar has effectively become the third canoni-cal sacred text in Judaism."

"May I ask, Rabbi, how you got the book?"

He rotated it in his hands, examining it in the light. "It's ac-tually a pretty good story," Kalman said. "The caretaker of a little synagogue up in Safed gave it to me. It must've been twenty, maybe twenty-five years ago. I was leading a tour of Israel for members of my part-time congregation. We were up in Safed, in the Galilee. After visiting the synagogue of Isaac Luria, the group had had enough of my history of Kabbalah and wanted to go shopping in the artists' quarter. So I wan-dered off down the hillside, alone. Within only a few blocks the buildings began to thin out and the narrow street became just a rocky, zigzag path down the side of the mountain.

That's when I noticed the entrance to the courtyard of a small Spanish-Portuguese-style synagogue. I was tired, the gate was ajar, and the place was deserted. So I walked in. . . ."

Kalman closed his eyes for a moment, recalling that old Mediterranean prayer hall. Its ceiling was high—easily two stories—and supported by four slightly pointed, white plastered arches that, in turn, rested upon columns. Each column was painted a bright, high-gloss blue. Most of the windows had bright blue curtains that billowed lazily with every passing breeze. The big stone blocks paving the floor had been worn to a shine by the foot-shuffle genuflections of generations of worshippers. Every inch of mortar between every block of pavement was also painted bright azure. The bottom half of all four walls was also a bright, high-gloss blue.

Blue: the color of the sea and the color of the sky. "And beneath God's feet was the likeness of sapphire stones, like the purity of the sky itself"—Exodus 24:10. And blue: the color associated with God's fleeting feminine presence.

The top half of the room and ceiling was white and festooned with a haphazard array of fluorescent lights, space heaters, bare incandescent bulbs, chandeliers, and sconces for candles, as well as an assortment of electric fans. The walls were interrupted regularly with cushioned benches and alcoves for bookshelves. Along the far wall were six high, narrow, arched windows. They had neither screens nor glass. Birds occasionally flew in and out. Rays of afternoon sunlight flitted across the prayer desks and bookshelves, igniting them, one after another, with flashes of white light. And in the center, several feet above floor level, stood an ornate pulpit surrounded by a turquoise railing.

"It was the most mysteriously beautiful place I think I've ever been in," said Kalman. "I just stood there, mesmerized by the sunlight and the twittering of the birds, when the caretaker, an old Moroccan-looking man, startled me out of my reverie. . . ."

"*Mincha* doesn't start for a few hours."

"What?"

"The afternoon service, it doesn't begin for a few hours."

"This is a beautiful synagogue."

"It needs a new roof; the plumbing's shot."

"What's it called?"

"The plumbing problem?"

"No, the synagogue."

"Benaiah, the Yosé Benaiah Synagogue."

"Who is Yosé Benaiah?"

"Third-century Talmudic teacher."

"I've never heard of him."

"We only have fragments."

"Such as?"

"Tractate *Ta'anit* 7a: 'If you occupy yourself with Torah for its own sake, your learning will become a source of life.' "

"Beautiful."

"My personal favorite is from tractate *Baba Batra*. It says that once Rabbi Benaiah came upon Abraham's burial cave. There, in front, standing guard, he found Abraham's servant, Eliezer. 'What is Abraham doing?' asked Benaiah. 'He and Sarah are making love,' said the servant."

"Visiting the caves of people who make love for eternity—an interesting character, this Benaiah guy."

"Maybe that's why they named the synagogue after him."

"What a wonderful story. Thank you. Say, you wouldn't by any chance know where I might find some old Kabbalistic books, would you?"

"Have you looked over there?" The old man gestured toward what looked like a pile of rubbish on a table in a darkened alcove. "Go ahead, help yourself."

"But when I walked over to the table," said Kalman, "I saw that it wasn't trash; it was a heap of old Hebrew books. Most of them were in pretty bad condition—individual pages, covers without contents, dozens of damaged prayer books. And that's when I noticed *this* book. I asked the caretaker if it was for sale."

"Doesn't belong to anyone now," he replied. "Go ahead, take it. It's yours. Has your name on it."

"I couldn't possibly—"

"Don't be silly. It's been lying there for years waiting for someone like you. If it will make you feel better, you can make a donation." He gestured toward a small wooden box by the door. Carved on it were the customary words *A gift given in secret.*

"I thanked him profusely," Kalman said, "stuffed a twenty-dollar bill into the slot, and walked back outside with the book you are holding."

The young woman looked at Kalman, then she looked down at the Zohar.

"Here," said Kalman. "You mentioned earlier that you had an epiphany. Let us learn something together from the Zohar about epiphanies." He opened the book to its first comment on Genesis. "It's a very famous passage; I've studied it many times before. Each time, I get something new."

"IN THE BEGINNING ..." The beginning of the Holy One's interpretation [of Scripture] was the scoring of a glyph in the supernal purity: a dark spark, a hardened flash of light. It issued from what is beyond comprehension, from the secret of the One without End.... Beyond that point, nothing can be known....

"That's pretty much how everything begins," Kalman reflected. "You wake up. Before you open your eyes, there is only a mirror-smooth sheet of unconscious ice. And then, from out of that nowhere—and it has to be a nowhere, because there are no coordinates—suddenly a pinprick of light. And the spark does only one thing. It chisels out a single mark, engraves one letter. And—whammo!—the unity is gone. Where once there was One, now there are galaxies and migrating birds, mitochondria swimming in our cellular protoplasm, giant Sequoias, refractor telescopes, that big red neon Tower Records sign down there across the street, and this mug of French roast Starbucks coffee that I picked up this morning on my way here."

The young woman reached into her bag for a notebook.

"Relax," said Kalman. "This is not the sort of thing you can or should write down. Trust your ability to absorb what's important. Remember, all the good stuff is already recorded in sacred text anyway."

"My first lesson?"

"That's not a bad place to begin. But it's not over yet." Scanning the page with his index finger: "This is how the paragraph concludes."

The name of this mystical novel will come from the Book of Daniel, where we read: "And those who understand will be radiant like the bright light . . ."

"The Hebrew for bright light or radiance is *Zohar*. . . ."

". . . streaming through a window in the sky, just as those who nurture others to righteousness will be like the starry firmament for ever and ever."

"You will notice," said Kalman, "that this sequence of ideas is not accidental. The author of the Zohar—whoever he was—begins his mystical novel the way God begins creation and the same way we all become conscious—with a dark spark, a cosmic seed. Only then do we get this Daniel passage about righteousness and radiance. Do you see? Awareness *initiates* being a good person; they are causally related. Reverence makes you a better human being.

"I have a friend out in Berkeley," Kalman continued, "who teaches photography. Every year he asks his students to name the first thing they saw that morning. He says they always think very carefully. One invariably says, the alarm clock; another, the pillow; and another, the tree outside her window—you know, things like that. And then he scolds them: 'No, no, no. *Before* you open your eyes!' "

The young woman's eyes were wide open. "I want to learn this," she said. "How do I begin?"

"Come," said Kalman, "let me walk you downstairs to meet a friend of mine in the admissions office. She'll set you up with all the catalogs and applications. But then I want you to go home and wait nine months."

"Nine months!"

"Otherwise, as the Hasidim say about any big, new idea, it might miscarry."

"Rabbi Stern," she said, "I've already waited nine years. . . ."

Kalman grinned. "All right, then, nine days."

They both laughed.

MANHATTAN

Kalman walked back upstairs, returned to his office, and picked up the 1647 Zohar to put back in its bubble-wrap envelope for safekeeping. Absentmindedly, the way he might have cleaned his eyeglasses, he slid his finger between two of the layers of its delaminating back cover—for no other reason than to see how far it might go. But, to his surprise, the old glue offered no resistance; his finger slid all the way in. With a barely audible crackle, the cardboard split in two, exposing the face of another page. But the face of the new page was not blank—it had handwriting on it! Kalman was dumbfounded. He might as well have been gazing at the rings of Saturn.

Before him were several sentences that seemed to be the text of some sort of journal entry or, perhaps, as he tried to decipher it, maybe a letter. Like the Zohar, they were in Aramaic:

השתא ידענא דהי ביגגא

דקרדינותא איזה זרעא

דנקודא דשיזרותא יהלי

עלכא דאתי איהו רחמא

דאיכא דמגיאותא האי ביגגא

דקרדינותא איהי גלכי

חנהירא עלמא דאתי אידי

רקיכא עילאה דלא התדבק

אלא דאלין יתרין אנטריט

לאתעביד חד את זושיכא אמא

גיגגא ביגגא דקרדינותא

יעלמא דאתי

משה בן שם טוב דחואדי

אל-חגרא

Now I understand. *Botzina d'qardinuta* is the seed point of beginning, and *alma d'ah-tay* is the mother-womb of being. *Botzina d'qardinuta*, he is the flash of light. *Alma d'ah-tay*, she is the unattainable and ultimate womb. But these two must become one. You are the darkness; I am the spark. *Botzina d'qardinuta* and *alma d'ah-tay*.

Moshe ben Shem Tov d'Vadi al-Hajra.

Kalman was suddenly aware of the pounding of his heart. "Letter. Letter. My God, in my hands . . . right, it's a letter . . . here. It's a love . . . goddamn letter, some kind of love letter. No, no, it's theology . . . some kind of Kabbalah . . . maybe. She loves me; no, she doesn't." He closed his eyes and took several deep breaths.

Kalman stared at the newborn page and whispered its word pairs: "*Botzina d'qardinuta* and *alma d'ah-tay*." To any student of the Zohar, these two phrases are shorthand for one of the Zohar's great insights into the ultimate nature of creation. *Botzina d'qardinuta*—literally a spark of impenetrable darkness—and *alma d'ah-tay*—literally the world that is coming—are, respectively, the father-spark of consciousness and the mother-womb of being. Professor Arthur Green once suggested that the dark spark is too subtle to be seen until it is reflected in the mirrored halls of the mother-womb, which, without the spark, would remain dark and unknowable. So *botzina d'qardinuta* and *alma d'ah-tay*, in other words, are not merely just any spark and any womb, they are *the* spark and *the* womb. And for traditional Judaism, in which God can have neither gender nor partner, because these phrases are obviously gendered and partners *within* God, they are therefore also potentially heretical.

Furthermore, to fully comprehend their relationship to each other is to solve the Zohar's—and Kabbalah's—abiding mystery: If God is all there is, then why did God make the world? And if God made the world, how did God do it? And if God is perfect, but the world is not, then what went wrong? They are, of course, all different ways of asking the same question. And whoever it was who wrote this page, this journal, this epistle, was therefore talking about the *raza d'razin*, the secret of secrets. And he wasn't talking about it in just the abstract, either. It seemed to Kalman that the author was trying to solve the mystery—right there, in the letter. But who was he? And why did he write it? And what was it doing for all these centuries glued inside the back cover of Kalman's 1647 Livorno Zohar? And, for that matter, why did it fall out *this* morning? Kalman looked at the page again and said to himself, "I can't do this one alone."

He picked up the phone and called Alexander Wasserhardt, a semiretired librarian and confidant. They had gotten to know each other back when Kalman was first trying to complete his dissertation and Wasserhardt worked in a book bindery. For the better part of a year, Kalman found himself more interested in learning how books were made than in reading what was in them. That's how he found Wasserhardt. Wasserhardt didn't write books, he *made* them. He bound them, repaired them, put them back together; he gave them new life. He had a whole room full of book-manufacturing machines and materials—binders, folders, stitchers, embossers, glue presses, stacks of cardboard, leather, paper, cloth.

Kalman had once asked him the purpose of those thin little brightly colored cloth strips at the top and bottom of a book's binding. Wasserhardt held up his necktie and waved it at him: "It makes you look more like a proper mensch, *nicht?*" When Kalman, as a graduate student, had learned that there was an opening at the rabbinic school's library, he got Alex an interview.

Wasserhardt was almost eighty years old now; the skin on the backs of his hands looked like crumpled waxed paper, his cheeks were covered with peach fuzz. Students told one another that it was the books that kept him going.

"Alex," said Kalman, "great, you're in. Don't go anywhere."

"And where would I go, *nu?* To a movie at eleven o'clock in the morning?"

"Important, it's . . . I have something. . . . Just stay put, Alex. I'll be down right—"

Kalman left without even closing the door to his office.

"This . . . Look at this . . . would you, Alex?" Kalman held up the Zohar.

"You want I should bind it for you?"

"No, Alex; it's not . . . not the book."

"Calm down, Kalman. *Jah,* here, sit right here in this chair," he said, patting the seat.

Kalman followed his instructions and, without trying to speak, carefully peeled apart the two halves of the cover, exposing the concealed page. He set it open on the desk.

The old man's eyes widened. Gently, reverently, he rotated the book so that it now faced him. Then he closed the two halves of the back cover and peeled them apart again for himself. "Where did you find this, *mein* Kalman? Do you think we could . . . maybe . . . ?" Removing a thin white plastic spatula from the back of the middle desk drawer, he cautiously jiggled it beneath the page. There was another series of faint crackles, and it was free of the book entirely: The two halves of the cover had borne a child. "Once the glue in one spot goes, it usually gives everywhere else, too," he whispered with satisfaction.

The old man began, slowly, examining the page.

Kalman craned his neck. "What are you looking for, Alex?"

"Wire lines and chain lines, maybe, if we're lucky, part of a watermark."

"Wire lines and chain lines?"

"*Jah.* If you look closely"—angling the page up in front of the lamp—"here, you can make out these thin little parallel lines. Do you see? They are a mirror image of the box frame in which they laid out the wet rag pulp. These are the wire marks. The wires, the horizontal lines, are kept separated, every so often, by a fine vertical chain. See?"

Kalman slid his fingers along the surface of the paper as if he were reading Braille.

"Maybe you heard of laid-finish paper?" said Wasserhardt. "That's where it comes from. They would *lay* the wet pulp on a screen of wires and little chains. The Moors, they brought the technology with them to Spain, and from there it spread all over Europe. And wire lines this far apart, I am pretty sure that makes it before the fifteenth century. Where did you say you got this?"

"The caretaker of a little synagogue in Safed gave it to me. It must have been at least twenty years ago. . . ."

"To have such a treasure for so long and not to know it . . ."

Wasserhardt sighed. "Well, one thing is for sure: It's older than the 1647 publication date of your Livorno Zohar."

"Really? How much?"

"Well, manuscript waste material was commonly used well into the sixteenth century. But I am guessing maybe even a few hundred years before that."

Kalman counted in his head. "Are you saying fourteenth century?"

"*Jah.* Maybe even earlier. See how thick the paper is and how irregular the laid lines are? I'm pretty sure they stopped making paper like that well before the fourteenth. I should show it to Rivkin."

"Rivkin?"

"Dovid Rivkin. He buys and sells rare books and manuscripts, dabbles in paleography, you know, ancient documents. But he's an old man—only comes in a few times a week. He's got this little shoebox of an office and a kid who does most of the work for him now. I think it's in the Chrysler Building. . . . *Jah,* the Chrysler Building, that's it. I've got his card here somewhere." Wasserhardt removed the rubber band from a stack of business cards and fanned them out like a riverboat gambler. "Here it is!" He squinted at the fine print. "He's what you should call a watermark man."

"A watermark man?"

"*Jah,* a watermark man. One time he showed me. He has catalogs and catalogs of watermarks that can tell when the paper was made. They find a watermark on the paper in a book with a publication date, and then they know that the paper is at least that old. And then they put it in the catalog."

"But we don't have a watermark."

"Well, maybe . . . we do. Do you see this little design?" He angled the paper so that Kalman could just make out on its edge what looked like what might be—with some *very* creative imagination—part of a horse. "Well, if, and it's a big if—*if* he can find the other half and recognize the image, and, *if* he can find it in one of his catalogs, and, *if*, in his catalog, it has been dated, he can pinpoint the century and maybe even the decade."

Wasserhardt held up the page again, this time to the window. "Ah-ha! Look here. Kalman, this is even better!"

Kalman leaned forward, craning his neck.

Above the text of the document, the paper was thinner, permitting more light to pass through; its surface was coarse.

Kalman nodded. "What is it?"

"An erasure!"

"So?"

"So, an erasure means that some words are missing."

"But it also means they're gone."

"Well, maybe not. Kalman, your page might be a palimpsest."

"A palimpsest?"

"A manuscript someone wrote on more than once. But the earlier strata of the writing might still be legible."

"How?"

"Sometimes, with ultraviolet light. The ink they used, it could leave chemical traces absorbed by the paper that you cannot see with your eyes. However, in light of other wavelengths and a good graphics . . . computer instructions? What do you call it?"

"A graphics program?"

"*Jah*, a graphics program. It is all very scientific. They compare the page with the photos they took under ultraviolet light, and sometimes they can read what used to be there."

"And where do we get some ultraviolet light?"

"Rivkin will know this kind of thing. Leave me the page and I will show it to him."

Kalman thought of all things he had erased and deleted over the course of his life. He was relieved that technicians of ultraviolet light were not widely available.

BOSTON

The first time Kalman actually saw another world was back in 1965, when he went on a field trip in Mr. Arnold Smolens's ninth-grade science class. Most of the kids in the class were more excited about being on the roof of a Harvard University building at night than astronomy and horsed around. They filed through the big metal doorway and out into the crisp November evening. Before them stood the gray-domed observatory. As they assembled inside, Mr. Smolens's graduate student friend gave a little speech about nocturnal eyesight, whereupon he switched off the white incandescent bulbs and turned on wire-caged red ones. Kalman was spellbound.

"This is a refractor telescope. It was built in 1912 by Alvan Clark and Sons with a nine-inch objective lens," said Mr.

Smolens. Then he picked up a metal box with three big buttons attached to a thick black electric cable. He pressed the bottom one. (Kalman still remembered that, after more than three decades.) There was a loud *kerchunk* and the whine of an electric motor, accompanied by the faint smell of ozone as a vertical slit in the roof slowly ground open, revealing a vertical slice of the night sky. Then Mr. Smolens pressed another button, and the dome with its slice of sky began to rotate.

"There, see it, Arnold?" whispered the grad student, lining up the long brass tube with the hole in the roof.

Smolens nodded. "Switch on the tracker."

"What's a tracker?" asked Kalman.

"Compensates for the earth's rotation—keeps the scope aimed at the same thing."

The two men maneuvered a wooden platform under the telescope, and the grad student went to work, first with the spotting scope and then with the fine-focus mechanism.

"Okay, kids, listen up," said Smolens. "Everyone gets a turn. Just be careful; even the pressure of your eye on this eyepiece here can wreck the focus. And whatever you do, don't bump the telescope itself."

Kalman was tenth in line. He removed his glasses and carefully lowered his eye to the lens. But all he could see was a black circle strewn with fuzzy white dots and a much larger one near the center with what looked like horns. "I think it's out of focus, Mr. S."

The teacher took Kalman's hand in the darkness, gently directing it to a small knob. Its mechanism was smooth, lubricated. Less than a quarter turn, and: "Unbelievable!" They weren't horns; they were the rings of Saturn! "I thought they were horns, Mr. S.," he whispered.

"So did the early astronomers, Kalman."

"Early navigators," explained the grad student, "believed the stars were all attached to the surface of a giant transparent rotating dome. Now we understand it's the earth that moves. From spectral analysis—that is, from examining the different colors of starlight—we are able to deduce that the stars are different distances away. Many of the brightest stars are actually galaxies, containing millions of stars. And as we move even farther away toward the event horizon of the universe, the stars seem to be uniformly distributed and of equal brilliance."

"What's beyond the event horizon?" asked Kalman.

"Remember when we talked about Einstein's theory of the big bang, Kal? Well, when Einstein said 'everything,' he meant 'everything.' Not just matter and energy, but space and time, too. If you could beat the speed of light and get your rocket ship all the way to the event horizon, you wouldn't see a sphere the size of the expanding universe. You would have also gone back in time. You would see only a point of light, a spark of infinite density containing everything yet to come—galaxies and planets, civilizations and centuries, people, everything—even the question you just asked. Everything!"

Kalman Stern just stood there gazing through that opening in the dome and into the starry firmament. He repeated his teacher's words: *a point of light . . . containing everything yet to come.* And for just one moment, the heavenly lights reciprocated his affections: They condensed themselves like a torrent gushed through the narrowing walls of a sluice. They slid through the slit in the nine-inch Alvan Clark refractor dome's open mouth. They squeezed themselves into a single spark of moistened light and planted a silent kiss on the lips of Kalman Stern. He swallowed hard and blinked, trying to clear his vision. He never told anyone about it. Even if he had wanted to, he didn't know how.

He wasn't aware of it then, of course, but that was also when he became a Kabbalist.

In 1940, Cities Service, a Tulsa oil company, erected a huge sign over its divisional office in the Peerless Auto Building on Beacon Street in Boston. They commissioned the University-Brink company to erect a sign in the shape of their logotype, which was then a shamrock. In 1965, when Cities Service changed its name, they had their sign rebuilt with the company's new red, blue, and white triangular logo. It measured sixty feet square, was electrified with 250 high-voltage transformers, and contained more than five miles of 5,878 glass tubes filled with neon gas. The big new double-sided sign said: CITGO. To this day, the Citgo sign in Kenmore Square is regarded as a prime example of neon urban art and has become a definitive Boston landmark.

It is also easily visible from across the Charles River in Cambridge and from the rooftops of many of the Harvard buildings there. But Kalman Stern did not initially notice the recently electrified sign. He was, after all, only fourteen years old at the time and preoccupied with other things.

MANHATTAN

Only a few minutes after leaving his unglued 1647 Zohar page with Alexander Wasserhardt, Kalman stopped in front of a cluttered NYU bulletin board. And right there, crammed in for the whole world to see, between a handwritten index card ("Seeking Roommate"), a purple-and-black poster heralding a student film festival, and an $8^{1}/_{2}$-by-11 canary yellow flyer about guitar lessons, was a handbill announcing a public lecture up at Columbia:

The New York Association for Astronomy and Cosmology. 7:30 p.m. Wednesday, September 17, 1997. "The Seed Point of Beginning: Some Recent Images from the Orbital Chandra X-ray Observatory Telescope Regarding Light in the Early Universe." Dr. Isabel Benveniste, Senior Research Astronomer. Pupin Hall, Columbia University, Room 100.

"The Seed Point of the Beginning," Kalman said to himself. "Son of a bitch." He pulled out his cell phone.

"Jonathan? Hello. . . . Yes, it's me, Stern, Kalman Stern. . . . Yes, everything's okay, but something has come up and I'm going to have to postpone our coffee date for this evening. We'll reschedule in class tomorrow, okay? Thanks for being so understanding." Kalman closed his cell phone and rummaged through the vest pocket of his jacket until he found the back of an envelope, upon which he recorded the lecture's time and place.

It was an exciting presentation; Kalman was glad he had come. He had long been fascinated by the similarities between Kabbalah and what little he knew of cosmology. And while he had never been among those who believed that Kabbalists were in possession of some esoteric, scientific wisdom—"God is not about science, nor is science about God," he had once said to a class—now, right here on the screen, in front of him, were some breathtaking images that effectively blurred most of the customary distinctions between mystical experience and scientific evidence.

"My God," he said to himself, "these pictures could pass for illustrations of Ezekiel's psychedelic vision of the chariot."

Using cutting-edge technology, the lecturer kept coming up with statements that might have been written by a thirteenth-century Kabbalist. She stepped out from behind the podium and clicked on a penlike gizmo that shone a thin red beam of light onto the screen. "Would you look at these." She spoke with an enthusiasm bordering on rapture. During the question-and-answer period that followed, Kalman wrote out one of his own.

"Yes," said the lecturer, pointing to him. "The gentleman in the back."

Kalman stood up. "It is my understanding that current scientific thinking remains undecided about whether light is a particle or a wave. In view of what you've just said, Dr. Benveniste, would that always have been the case? I mean, do we think that light has always been the same, or has it changed? When we see these images, are we looking at particles or waves?" He sat back down.

She nodded. "It's a wonderful question, but I am afraid, sir, that my answer will probably be disappointing. It's both." She then spoke at some length. And even though he tried to pay close attention and nodded frequently so that she and the rest of the audience would think he understood the answer, Kalman's thoughts drifted. He wondered what she would be like as a dinner companion. His was the last question of the evening.

When it was over, Kalman picked up one of the handouts listing all the lectures in the series. He wanted to make sure he had the correct spelling of her last name: Benveniste. Now, there's an apt name for an astronomer, he thought: "a good view." Well, maybe if she would lose those Coke-bottle eyeglasses, Benveniste could also mean "looks good."

It was a clear autumn evening and definitely too nice for the subway. Besides, after the talk, he wanted access to the night sky. Even if he couldn't see the stars through the neon glare, he liked the thought that there was nothing separating him from the heavens. "On a clear night and without the pollution of other light sources," the astronomer had said, "the human eye can discern only about six thousand stars."

So he started out down Broadway. He watched a gaggle of taxis race by and two kids sharing a joint and an old woman carrying her possessions in three big green plastic trash bags and an Asian man who looked like Ho Chi Minh hosing down the sidewalk in front of his flower shop and a young couple holding hands like they were Adam and Eve, and he wondered if, when his grandfather Herschel first arrived in the Port of New York in 1903, he, too, ever savored such evenings of wonderment.

At the next intersection, Kalman walked over to the island in the middle of the boulevard and sat down on an empty bench. He looked up toward all the stars he could not see.

"I want," he said to himself, "I want to know the truth. I want to know what it all is supposed to mean. I don't want some secret number code or a weird Kabbalistic diagram. I am forty-six years old, and I want to know why I am alive. And I want to know what I'm supposed to do with my life. I want to know why light is a particle and a wave. And what that astronomer looks like without her glasses. I want to know why when I get excited my syntax goes all to hell. And just who did write *The Book of Love*, anyway? And I want a sign, yes, I want some kind of sign, an indication that I'm at least on the right track. And I'd like to have a mystical experience just once before I die. . . ."

· Two ·

CASTILE

By 1260, King Alfonso X of León and Castile had extended the Christian *reconquista* throughout most of the Iberian Peninsula. All that now remained of Muslim power was the southern coastal Almohad kingdom of Granada. Like Spanish kings before him, Alfonso the Wise, or El Sabio, realized he could free his troops for service elsewhere by persuading Jews to colonize his newly conquered territories. Through royal edicts, Jews were granted religious freedom and privileged residences. And since Jews were also unable to hold political power or align themselves with either nobility or church, they became natural allies of the crown. This did not, however, foster the warmest of relations with the church.

As was the case throughout most of medieval Europe, Jewish existence depended on a precarious and perpetually shifting balance between privilege and privation. Even though, for instance, it was forbidden to disturb the Jews during their observance of the Sabbath, the number of synagogues was limited by law. To help prevent the possibility of blood libels—wherein Jews were accused of using the blood of Christian children in the preparation of Passover matzah—Jews were forbidden to leave their homes during Easter. Or, while forced conversions of Jews into Christianity were illegal, converting to Judaism was a capital offense. Pope Clement IV gave the Inquisition carte blanche to pursue any Christian suspected of practicing Judaism or any Jew accused of exercising unreasonable influence over Christians, which effectively included everyone. Jews were compelled to carry a special badge identifying them as Jews. Massacres were common.

Despite all this, Jews parlayed their position with finesse. And, as they had under Muslim rulers previously, Jews in Christian Spain gradually rose to the highest positions of administration and finance. By 1294, for example, nearly one-quarter of the total Castilian income came from Jews. Even despite mounting hostility, the state was naturally reluctant to part with such revenue. Jewish courtiers and, with them, much of the highest strata of Jewish society gradually assimilated into the larger community. Jewish jurisprudence, literature, and philosophy flourished.

One vignette is particularly instructive: For four days in July of 1263, the port city of Barcelona was the scene of a formal and public debate between an apostate Jew and Rabbi Moses ben

Nahman, or, as he is more commonly known by the acronym of his initials, the Ramban—arguably the ranking rabbi of his generation. The contest was held in the presence of King James of Catalonia himself, with the Dominican friars at his side. This was probably the last time in the Middle Ages when the Jewish spokesman at such a disputation was permitted to speak freely. But the Ramban did just a little too well. Instead of declaring the Ramban victorious, the Dominican fathers called off the contest and subsequently had him convicted of attacking Christianity. The matter went all the way to Rome, and only after an intervention by the king was the Ramban granted an indefinite postponement. Ultimately, however, he was compelled to leave his family and flee to Israel.

"Perhaps it is not such a victory after all," said Don Moshe ben Shem Tov de Guadalajara.

"Please lower your voice, señor," said an older man at the next table, gesturing with a sweep of his hand toward the book-lined walls.

"Forgive me, I did not realize I was speaking loudly." Then, in a whisper, leaning forward: "Yosef, if you win, you lose."

"Anyone can win so that everyone knows it," said Don de Guadalajara's friend, wiping the sweat from his forehead and the back of his neck. "The trick is, can you win so that people only realize it much later? Jews must never *appear* to win. The world will not tolerate it."

"How, of all people, could the Ramban have been so naive?

He must have inadvertently betrayed his pride when the contest was done."

"In front of the king himself, who would not look happy?" said Yosef.

"But he should have at least acted like he was injured. You know, mortally wounded—let them lead him, disconsolate, from the hall."

"He should have stayed with philosophy and not tried to be so erudite with Kabbalah."

"How do you know he tried Kabbalah?" Moshe ben Shem Tov de Guadalajara edged forward on his chair.

And in this way the discussion reverted, as it so frequently did, to philosophy versus Kabbalah. Even though Yosef had authored important books of Kabbalah himself, he returned increasingly to more rational philosophy. But de Guadalajara invariably tilted toward intuition, paradox, and the esoteric. Their friendship and this afternoon's argument typified much of mid-thirteenth-century Jewish intellectual Spanish life.

Don de Guadalajara reached into a leather satchel, brought out a sheaf of pages, and slid them carefully across the table.

"More? You have more?" said his friend, eyes opening wide.

"Oh yes, there are scores of sections."

His friend leaned forward and whispered, "Moshe, when can I see them for myself?"

"But surely, Yosef, you would not ask me to violate my oath? I swore to the old man that I would guard them with my life and show others *only* what I had faithfully copied."

Yosef untied the twine, carefully opened the first leaf, and read for several minutes. "This is wonderful, Moshe," he said, looking up. "Simply amazing. I have never read anything like it before. May I take it home with me, just for one night?"

"Do not insult me, my friend. I insist: Keep it. Do you see, I have already written your name on the back: Yosef Gikatilla."

"But I could not do this."

"Nonsense. I can make as many copies as I like. But promise me: You will tell *anyone* who asks that you had to pay a very handsome price. And do not forget to tell him *from whom* you received it."

"How can you go on supporting yourself like this?"

"Do not worry. I have arranged another source of income."

"*Another* source?"

"Yes, I have a new student who pays very, *very* well."

"But tutoring will only take *more* time from your work. Tell me—this student of yours, is he any good? Does he show promise?"

"You do not understand. The student is not a he."

"Not a he?!"

"The student is a señora."

"A señora? But surely you are making a joke at my expense."

"No. This one is a Jew. Sometimes she asks even better questions than you do. So help me, Yosef, if she were a man, I swear, I would take her to Gerona to meet Yitzhak."

"And her husband, is he not jealous?"

"Her husband is one of El Sabio's closest financial advisers. He and his entire family summer with the king right here in Valladolid."

"I do not understand. Why would he not be jealous?"

"Because he is the one who hired me."

"Moshe . . ."

"Yes?"

"A man does not get that influential by simply donating to charity. You would please exercise the greatest of caution—just for me, please. A man that powerful . . ."

Moshe was short—barely five feet tall. Even worse, God—who has never been accused of not having a sense of humor—had also endowed him with the wiry physique of a gymnast. Just what the Jews of thirteenth-century Castile did *not* need: a five-foot-one-inch acrobat. Once, when he was still a boy, he had horrified his parents by demonstrating that he could support three of his classmates while they, locking arms, perched themselves precariously on his hips and shoulders. "It is an upside-down pyramid," declared one. "Its top is on earth, and its base is up in the sky!"

"It is not strength, Mother," he said in self-defense. "It is all balance. I am sure that if I could get the balance right, I could hold ten people."

But she only moaned, "Jews, Moshe, do not belong in the circus. You are such a good boy, why must you always be into such mischief?"

His father scowled. "It will be a miracle if someday you can just manage to support a wife and family."

The expression on young Moshe's face only exacerbated such exchanges. No matter how he tried to alter it, Moshe ben Shem Tov's face bore the involuntary grimace of duplicity. Even now, after four decades of life, his default facial expression still had the faint but unmistakable smile of a man who had something to hide. For as long as he could remember, people simply assumed he was up to no good. No matter how blameless he had been, a perpetually upward curl on the corners of his lips and dark, deep-set eyes convinced even the most gullible interlocutor that Moshe must certainly be guilty of some recent deception.

This was not necessarily a problem when it came to romance, however. Women seemed only impressed by how well they imagined that a man with such a face could keep a secret or, even better, just what sort of a secret he might be keeping. They admired his discretion, his jet black hair and dark eyes, the apparent strength in his forearms, his way with words, and, above all, that perpetual, involuntary smile. Here was a man who would keep *their* secrets.

"I *did not* do it," he would protest.

"Oh, Don de Guadalajara, you are *so* discreet."

"That is because there is *nothing* to be discreet about," he would protest.

"Surely you can tell *me.*"

"There is nothing to *tell*," he would protest.

"Of course, of course, I understand. It will remain *our* secret."

"There is *no* secret," he would protest.

But it was no use. They would only smile demurely and fan themselves. The more forward might even accidentally brush the back of his hand. Or was it a caress?

Everyone always thinking you are up to mischief—it can do strange things to a man's way of looking at the world. In Moshe's case, it had two not unpredictable results: He became

passionately, even fanatically, righteous; and he became convinced that *other* people were concealing something *from him*. If
they looked innocent, he suspected they might be guilty. If
they appeared to be dishonest, he imagined they might be
telling the truth. If something looked ugly, he tried to see what
was beautiful inside; if it looked beautiful, he was suspicious.
For Moshe ben Shem Tov de Guadalajara, creation was latent
with layers of mystery. His was a world of secrets. Nothing
was the way it appeared.

"Successful human intercourse," he once opined to a friend
(who did not know whether to believe him or not), "is essentially the business of concealing more than what you reveal.
Those who become skilled at it succeed in all their endeavors.
Why, for example, when people first feel the stirrings of love
for each other, do they not understand that you must never
confess your love too soon? Why is it that seasoned business-
men always tell the truth, but never one word more than what
is required? Why is it that you cannot simply tell someone a
great religious truth without a whole rigmarole of questions
and hints, allusions and mysteries? I will tell you," he said. "It is
because that is the way God made the world."

Had there been gambling casinos in thirteenth-century
Castile, with such a face Moshe might have done well at the
poker table. But, alas, gambling casinos did not appear in
Western civilization until much later. Moshe might have
made a decent living as an actor, but the only successful theater
troupe in all of the Iberian Peninsula in the thirteenth century
was in Madrid, and they already had a long waiting list of
would-be thespians. He might even have made it as—how

shall we say it discreetly?—a ladies' man. They certainly swooned for his strength and his apparent facility with secrecy. But he was too shy. So Moshe ben Shem Tov de Guadalajara became a Kabbalist, a mystery writer, a fabulist, a recounter of the recondite.

To be truthful, even the process through which he recorded his words remained a mystery. Sometimes, when he wrote long into the night, he suspected that his words were not his own. He imagined that his hand had become the instrument of someone else—some hidden and, as yet, unnamed and ancient identity. And when the writing was done, he would sit and stare at the page of words, wondering who had written them.

SAFED: SECOND ITERATION

According to Jewish tradition, damaged or even irreparably worn holy books may not be destroyed. Instead they're either buried in a special cemetery crypt or stored away in the cellar of the synagogue along with other pieces of junk and building materials in a room called the *geniza*. The Hebrew root *ganaz* means "to hide." Indeed, one of the greatest bibliographic finds of the last century was the discovery of just such a storage room in the cellar of the great synagogue of Cairo. Its contents had been buried under the routine debris left by workmen over centuries. The latest inventory of these texts and fragments includes hundreds of thousands of entries. The collection is especially valuable, of course, because the expulsion of the Jews from Spain and the Inquisition destroyed virtually everything the Jews printed. How ironic. Books that in their time were too worn to use wind up being preserved, while the ravages of time, insects, and persecutions destroy all their younger and healthier relatives.

"Stern," said Slomovitz, looking up from his veggie burger, "how *did* you get this delaminating 1647 Livorno Zohar, anyway?" They were having lunch at an outdoor café on Lafayette Street.

"I told you, Milt, some old guy gave it to me."

"Where? Kalman. In a used-book store in Williamsburg? At the Port Authority bus station? A brothel in Tijuana? Really, how'd you get it?"

When Milton Slomovitz wasn't teaching medieval history at NYU, he was in his late sixties. But when he was teaching, he was twenty-three, maybe twenty-four. He had neatly combed, thinning white hair and always wore a necktie, always. He and Kalman were close friends. But this did not stop them from routinely teasing each other about their respective disciplines and how to maintain the proper balance between reason and emotion. Slomovitz was a Litvak—and proud of it. That is to say, Slomovitz took pleasure in knowing that he was of Lithuanian descent, where rationality was prized high above emotion. And he mischievously delighted, as a gesture of self-reaffirmation, in his conspicuous disdain for the emotional excesses of the Hasidic folk mystics of Poland and Galicia of which Kalman Stern was both a student and a teacher.

"Okay, okay, Milton, I'll tell you the whole thing. I was in Safed at the Yosé Benaiah Synagogue. Not many people go there; it's off the tourist circuit, way down the hill. It was hot, and I had sat down to enjoy the view and pretend I was living in the sixteenth century."

"One of my favorite centuries . . ."

"No one else was there but the caretaker. I asked him if he knew where there were any old Hebrew books, before they were consigned to the *geniza*. 'The *geniza*?' He only laughed. 'This whole building's a *geniza*. Is there some specific topic . . . ?'

" 'I am particularly interested in Kabbalah.'

" 'In that case,' he said, 'perhaps you'd prefer something from the seventeenth century.' He walked over to a dimly lit alcove where there was a pile of rubbish—old newspapers, an empty paint can, crumpled pages, pieces of lumber, torn maps, and the vital organs of several books. 'Here is some interesting material. . . .' He swatted away a paper coffee cup from the top of the pile of debris.

" 'Ah, yes,' he said, sneezing. He stooped down and retrieved an old book. He blew off some dust and opened it to the first page. Then, he read— Milt, I still remember the words. . . .

" '*Botzina d'qardinuta*.' He squinted, angled the page to catch more light, and then: '*Alma d'ah-tay*.'

"You know what they mean, Milt? 'A dark spark' and 'the world that's coming.' He read those words from the book. 'They're a pair,' the old guy said. 'The papa and the mama. They are everywhere. According to the Kabbalists, young man, the beginning of creation is a dimensionless point, called *botzina d'qardinuta*. It's a pinprick of light reflecting throughout the mirrored chambers of *alma d'ah-tay*, the world that is coming. Creation, you see, is not an event accomplished by God at some specific time in the past—*Deus abscondus!*' Then he looked right at me, Milt, so help me God. I remember it like it was yesterday. He said: 'Creation is *now*—wherever you look, this very moment. This is one of the great teachings of the Zohar: As we become conscious, we understand that creation is ubiquitous and continuous. Now there's Kabbalah for you,' he said. 'None of this silly spiritual prattle. They don't write stuff like that anymore.'"

"Stern, you are making this up," Milton finally interrupted.

"Milton, I may be a good storyteller, but this goes beyond even my imagination. But wait, there's more. As if I needed convincing, he handed me the book. 'Where did you get this?' I asked. 'It must be hundreds of years old.' With a wave of his hand, he merely gestured back toward the trash heap in an alcove: 'Seventeenth century, yessiree.'

" 'It's not the seventeenth century,' I said, 'it's just a pile of rubbish.'

" 'Only when you don't know where to look.'

" 'Go ahead,' the old man said. 'Open the book and see for yourself. It's got *your* name on it.'"

Slomovitz set down his burger.

"So I opened it to the title page. And there, along with a few other handwritten names, was Kalynomous ben Mazal—my name!

" 'This is *my* name!' I said to the caretaker. 'Who wrote it here?'

" 'Some things, if you understand what I mean,' he said, 'they just have your name on them. Most people are too busy to notice. Always keep your eye out for something with your name on it.' "

"Stern," said Slomovitz, "you have a dangerously fertile imagination."

"That's what I thought, too. I figured it must have been the heat. But that evening back at the hotel, I was still holding the old book in my hands. And my name—all right, I concede, it's not *that* uncommon—was really handwritten on the title page."

"So what did you do?" said Slomovitz.

"What would *you* do? I went back the next morning just as the service was ending. A few men were wrapping up their tefillin and folding their tallisim. Within a few minutes, most had hurried off up the hill. The only one left was a well-dressed middle-aged guy who seemed to be measuring one of the bookshelves with a tape."

" 'Excuse me,' I said. 'Do you know where I might find the caretaker?'

" 'Caretaker?' he says. 'Just look at this place—rubbish everywhere. It's a mess. It hasn't been cleaned for decades, maybe centuries.'

" 'But where is he?'

" 'Who?'

" 'The *shammas*.'

" 'There is no caretaker here. They can't afford one.' Then, after removing what turned out to be an empty cigarette pack from his shirt pocket, he crumpled it up and tossed it into a corner of the seventeenth century. 'You got a cigarette?'

" 'Sorry, I don't smoke.'

"I walked over to the pile of trash and papers in the corner and stooped down to get a closer look. But it was only rubbish."

"Stern," said Slomovitz, "you should write a novel—not history, not theology, not even a memoir, but a novel. Do you see what happens when even a fine mind is immersed for too long in the Kabbalah?"

"Milton, it's the truth, so help me. . . ."

"Stern, you should be in a mental institution." He motioned to the waiter for the check. "Let me take it; you're going to need all the money you can get. Decent psychiatric hospitals cost an arm and a leg nowadays."

Kalman laughed. "This whole city is one big psychiatric hospital, Milton."

"But I love it. I could never leave."

The waiter brought the check. Slomovitz slid a twenty-dollar bill under the sugar bowl and stood up. "I thought there were only forty-nine million stories about the Kabbalah, Stern," he said, "but you just told me another."

CASTILE

This particular señora was married to a renowned financier and one of the more influential Jews in the court of King Alfonso the Wise. It was, however and alas, an arranged marriage that had yielded neither fruit nor, truth be told, much passion. The señora's black—and now a few gray—curls and a height of nearly six feet gave her a statuesque dignity. Even though she was well into her fifties, men still turned their heads.

The señora and her husband were about to receive an old family friend, just returned from Majorca on some kind of diplomatic errand for the king. After recounting his adventures and sharing some wine and fruit, their visitor set a small bundle on the table. "I have something here I think you will find of interest, Judah."

He carefully opened a cloth pouch, producing an ornate brass mechanism composed of engraved rotating disks. The whole contraption was less than two handbreadths in diameter. On top of the base disk was a second, smaller, open-patterned one and, above it, what looked like a long, narrow stick or arrow, both of which were fixed so that they rotated on a central pin. The señora was unable to take her eyes off the shiny metal instrument on the table.

"It is an astrolabe," said their guest. "I got it from a compass maker on the island; the place is a center for cartographers and navigators. With this instrument, Judah, all you need is the location of two constellations, and you can have both a plane image of the celestial sphere and you can identify all the principal circles—the ecliptic, the celestial equator, and the Tropics of Cancer and Capricorn."

Don Judah's wife was mesmerized. "I do not understand," she whispered.

"I have heard of them before, my dear. Mariners use them. It is a device that can tell you where you are on the earth in relation to the heavenly spheres.

"But how," he said, turning to their friend, "could one instru-

ment possibly acquire so much information? Tell us, please,
how it works."

"This base brass plate is called the mater. Each one of these
inscribed lines on it represents celestial coordinates. The rotating, open-patterned disk above it is the rete. See, it contains
a map of the stars that rotate around the north celestial pole."
Then, pointing to the central pin: "All you need to do is align
this alidade straight rule here with a celestial object." He held
it up to his eye, as if sighting an imaginary star. "If you are in a
different latitude, you merely insert a different plate between
the mater and the rete. It's ingenious, brilliant. With it, the
heavens are yours!"

Don Judah rose, motioning for his guest to follow him to his
study for brandy.

Barely had the door closed behind the two men than the
woman was at the table, examining the instrument. She took
it in her hands, walked to the window, and held it up to one
eye. She still did not understand how it worked, but just
knowing what it could do was strangely thrilling. She walked
to another window, and in what, in the months ahead, would
become almost a religious ritual for her, she aimed it on the
distant hills. Then she held it toward the sky, looking for the
moon.

On the street below, a short, itinerant teacher of Kabbalah, in
a religious ritual of his own, made his way up the hill, past the
water trough, and toward the synagogue for afternoon prayers.
Preoccupied with the astrolabe, the señora noticed him only
obliquely.

"Judah," she said to her husband later that evening when they were alone, "I would very much like to learn how to read the holy language."

Don Judah was stunned, flabbergasted. "But, but women, my love, women do *not* read Hebrew."

"I know that, and I do not care. I want to know more about the heavens. I want to know about the spheres that govern the sublunar world. I want to know about eternity. And I want to be able to read the language of the words that contain the answers. Judah, does not the Torah itself say that God created the world by speaking it into existence: 'And God said, Let there be . . . And there was . . .' Please, Judah. No one will ever need to know. Oh, please . . ."

He thought for several minutes. She knew he was weighing the implications of such a decision. She had watched him in similar silences untangle difficult financial problems. Finally, after what seemed to her like an age, he smiled in satisfaction. "Very well," he said, "you shall have for yourself a teacher of Hebrew."

"Oh, thank you, Judah. Thank you!"

He kissed her cheek. "Just last month, at the conclusion of the morning service, Rabino Sanchez introduced me to a Kabbalist from Guadalajara whom he lauded as an excellent scholar and a fine teacher. Sanchez told me, later, that the man was also in need of financial assistance. So now, it seems, through your request, he will receive his charity with dignity."

She smiled.

"But no one, save the teacher and the members of this household, will know. Do you understand what I am saying?"

And she nodded in agreement.

MANHATTAN

Of all the varieties of Jewish mysticism, Kabbalah is the most fully developed and certainly the most well-known. Most historians agree that it attains maturity as a thirteenth-century Spanish system of theosophy claiming to explain the influence of human action on the inner workings of God. According to Kabbalah, human experience, the unfolding of world history, even the laws of nature themselves, are all manifestations of the divine psyche.

Scholarly consensus holds that these ideas first made their appearance in Provence. From southern France, they spread west to Gerona and then throughout most of the Iberian Peninsula. Kabbalistic thought reached its zenith a century later with the appearance of what is now known as the Zohar. Its author was purported to be none other than the renowned second-century mystic Shimon bar Yohai. Indeed, the faithful even today still believe that. It seems fitting that the authorship of the Zohar should remain mysterious.

Spain in that time was a fertile broth of religious ideas—Judaism, Christianity, Islam, philosophy, mysticism, Gnosticism. The countryside was rife with teachers and seekers. One of them, Yosef ben Avraham Gikatilla, was the author of the classic *Gates of Light*. It's an explanation of Kabbalistic symbolism and *sefirot*—the inner dimensions of the divine psyche. Another, his good friend Moshe ben Shem Tov de Leon, was a literary and mystical genius. For years he wandered among the towns of Castile, immersing himself in the traditions of the Geronese Kabbalists. We know also that, at least until 1291, Moshe ben Shem Tov resided in Guadalajara. By the final decade of that century, Moshe had become an itinerant teacher. He settled in the town of Ávila, where he devoted himself to circulating copies of what would come to be known as the Zohar. De Leon died in 1305. Was it during a mystical trance? Perhaps he ascended to heaven in a fiery chariot? Maybe it was due to purely natural causes. Or, God forbid, maybe he was murdered by a jealous husband? We do not know.

The faculty dinner that evening ran late. By the time Kalman walked outside, it was already dark; the pavement was still wet from rain. A few stragglers scurried by, hoping to make it up to Grand Central or Penn Station in time for the last express. Kalman turned west on Fourth Street, heading through NYU and toward the Sixth Avenue subway. Lost in thought, he did not notice the woman standing on the curb a few feet away, trying to hail a taxi. A van splashed through a puddle and she jumped backward, but not before taking a direct hit from the water in the pothole.

"Damn!" she hissed under her breath.

"You all right?"

"Wet. Just wet." She started to turn away.

"Excuse me, but did you give a lecture up at Columbia last week? Benveniste?"

And, with a cautious eye: "Yes."

"I was the guy who asked about light being a wave or a particle. . . ."

Silence. Then: "You were in the back, on the right?"

"Yes. My name is Kalman Stern."

She looked taller, more severe, off the podium. What little makeup she wore was perfect; her black curly hair fell flawlessly about her face.

"Those slides were really incredible. I had no idea. . . ."

She took a step backward.

"I'm sorry. Please forgive me. I teach mysticism." He fumbled in his jacket pocket and produced a business card.

"Oh," said the astronomer. "A rabbi?"

"Yes. Are you Jewish? Benveniste, it's an old Spanish Jewish name."

"No. As a matter of fact, I am a lapsed Catholic."

"Look, you're all wet. Here, take my, my handkerchief."

"It's nothing, thank you. I'm fine."

"No, please, really."

Then, to their mutual surprise, and against every rule of street smarts, as if they had known each other for decades, she matter-of-factly handed him her briefcase, raised the shoulder strap of her bag higher on her other shoulder so it wouldn't slip off, and accepted his white square cloth offering.

"You know, I saw this once before," she said.

"You mean déjà vu?"

"No, this scene happened to Doris Day and Cary Grant."

"I don't understand."

"In a movie, *That Touch of Mink*. She gets splashed by his

Rolls-Royce, and he sends his assistant, Gig Young, to pay the cleaning bill."

"Rolls-Royce . . . ?" He mentally opened one of half a dozen small wooden boxes and removed one of its index cards, upon which were written the director, actors, and plot summary of each movie he'd seen until he went off to college. His anxiety vanished. "Oh, you mean Cathy Timberlake and Philip Shayne. So that's why I wrote those cards. . . ."

"What cards?"

"That was their names."

"Whose?"

"Doris Day's and Cary Grant's."

"How did *you* know that?"

"Kid. When I was a kid, I was going to be a movie critic. I had an index card for every movie I'd ever seen."

She regarded him for a moment, then said, "Why, that is marvelous—simply marvelous."

"You know," he said, "I had to pay the driver of that van twenty bucks."

She could not conceal a cautious smile.

"Look, my handkerchief you can keep, but ask . . . I get to ask you questions . . . a few more . . . about what you talked about last week, okay . . . is that okay?"

She gave him a longer look. "Very well, but I will make you a counterproposition. We shall have a cup of coffee at the Time Cafe over on Lafayette, and I shall try to answer your questions. But in repayment, *Rabbi* Stern, you must tell me about bar mitzvahs."

"Okay . . . sure. Do I get to ask why?"

"In three weeks—I am aware that this may sound a little odd—I have been invited to attend a bar mitzvah at a big temple up on the West Side for the son of the head of my department."

"Mazel tov! But I still don't understand."

"Well, you see, I've never been to one; I don't know what to do."

"You haven't missed all that much."

"I'm supposed to do something—the word is *galley*, or *Galilee*, or—"

"You mean *Ga-lee-lah?*"

"Yes, *Ga-lee-lah*. That sounds like it. Well, Rabbi Stern, I don't have the slightest clue what that means. My boss keeps assuring me that I won't have to say anything in Hebrew or even English, but I still would like to know what the word *Ga-lee-lah* means."

"Beginning of time, how to dress a scroll of the Torah . . ."

Seated at the café, Kalman tried to relax by telling a joke.

"So there are these two old Jews who are obsessed with knowing what happens after you die," he said, putting his fork into a slice of coconut cream pie. "They swear a solemn oath that, God forbid, whoever dies first will stop at nothing to contact the one who survives. Moishe dies. Yonkel sits shivah, says kaddish for eleven months . . ."

"Shivah? Kaddish?"

"Jewish mourning rituals. But nothing happens. Then, after a few years, one evening the phone rings. It's Moishe!

" 'Moishe, is that you?'

" 'Yes, it's me, but I can't talk long.'

" 'So then quick, tell me, what's it like?' asks Yonkel.

" 'Oh, it's wonderful here. I sleep late, have a big breakfast, and then I make love. If the weather's nice, I usually go out into the fields and make love again. I come back inside for lunch and take a nap. Then I go out into the fields and make love, sometimes twice. I have a big dinner, and then, most evenings, I go out into the fields again and make love. Then I come inside and go to sleep.'

" 'And that's heaven!?' Yonkel gasps.

" 'Heaven?' says Moishe. 'Who said anything about heaven? I'm a rabbit in Minnesota!' "

It worked. Dr. Isabel Benveniste demurely covered her mouth with her napkin and laughed; her eyes twinkled behind her thick glasses.

Neither of them spoke for a few moments, then she said, "Kalman, may I ask you a personal question? I've been wondering about it since we met. Why did you become a rabbi?"

"For the money."

"No, really."

"Well, your question is often a euphemism for 'Why on earth would anyone in his right mind want to earn a living like that?' But a trapeze artist you don't ask, or a podiatrist, or a prostitute—only people who devote themselves to helping others try to find meaning in their lives. The real question, I've always thought, should be 'Why doesn't *everyone* want to be a rabbi, or a minister, or a priest?' What more fulfilling way could there be for someone to spend a life? I became a rabbi because a rabbi gets to be there when life seems to be coming apart or coming back together. He's the one who is supposed to know how to help find the meaning of life. In my case, there's only one problem. After decades, I still don't know anything more about it than when I walked into rabbinic school."

She was captivated by what he said and, especially, by the peculiar way he spoke when he got excited. He sounded so intent and earnest—as if he were too excited to be bothered with the rules of ordinary syntax. She removed a tissue from her purse and cleaned her glasses. "Kalman," she said, smiling, "rabbis preach sermons, right?"

Kalman nodded.

"Well, I'm curious. Do you write out your sermons, or do you give them without notes?"

"Every single word is right there in front of me on a piece of paper."

"I would have thought that a man with your command of language would find preaching from a text too constraining."

Kalman shrugged and looked away. "Mostly I preach variations of the same three sermons over and over again."

She frowned.

"No, I'm serious. Sure, there are a lot of variations, but that's all any preacher has, three basic sermons."

"For example?"

"Well, many of mine are about mysticism and how everything is connected, so I guess you could say they're about why we are here and what life means."

"Are you a mystic?"

"People become mystics, Professor Benveniste, for one of three reasons: because they've had a mystical experience, because they want one, or because they've fallen in love."

"You didn't answer my question."

"I write books with mysticism in the subtitle. Does that count?"

"Can you at least tell me what mysticism is?"

He closed his eyes as if he were trying to come up with a new and honest answer. "Mysticism," he said, "is the taking of more and more into your field of vision until there is nothing left outside—not even the one who is looking. Something like that."

"But surely no one could be in such a place *all the time?*"

"Correct. It's like breathing pure oxygen—you'd die of old age in ten minutes. Kabbalists explain it like this. There are two modes of being, if you will, two worlds. There's the World of Separation, this one that we inhabit most of the time, with its myriad array of discrete, finite, and seemingly independent parts, each with its own name, location, and, if it's human, its own agenda. Then there's the World of Unity, a radical monism, where there are no parts, no boundaries, and no names. There, everything is all one, or, more accurately, everything is the One. But the World of Separation abides *within* the bosom of the World of Unity. The best way I've ever found to explain it is an image I first heard from Daniel Matt, translator of the Zohar into English. He once explained that we have a word for leaf, twig, branch, trunk, roots. The words make it easier for us to categorize and comprehend reality. But we must not think that just because we have words for all the parts of a tree, a tree really has all those parts. The leaf does not know, for instance, when it stops being a leaf and becomes a twig. And the trunk is not aware that it has stopped being a trunk and has become the roots. Indeed, the roots do not know when they stop being roots and become soil, nor the soil the moisture, nor the moisture the atmosphere, nor the atmosphere the sunlight. All our names are arbitrarily superimposed on what is, in truth, the seamless unity of all being. And that is when the World of Separation gives way to the World of Unity. It lasts for only a moment, the twinkling of an eye. Then it's gone and we're bounced back into this World of Separation."

"I feel that way sometimes when I look at the heavens."

"So, may I ask what drew *you* to astronomy?"

"Oh, that's easy. When I was a little girl, our family used to spend summers on an island off the coast of Maine. I was a cautious child—still am. I used to lie on my back on the lawn out behind our house and look up at the stars. I made up a game. I would try to imagine the lines that joined the stars into their constellations. I was only seven at the time, so I only knew a few. And once I could summon the image with all its points of light and invisible lines, I would ask, 'And who created you, Mrs. Bear? And who created you, Mr. Orion?'

"One evening my mother must have overheard. The memory is vivid, even now—the moist sea air, the smell of her perfume. She came outside and sat down beside me. 'Belle'—she always called me Belle—'it sounds like you're talking to the stars.' She ran her fingers through my hair and said that when she was a little girl she used to do the same thing. 'Belle, honey,' she said, 'I hope you never stop wondering who created them.' It's my most important memory of her."

"What a beautiful and holy story."

Isabel shrugged. "After she died, I stopped asking the question. Candidly, I had forgotten all about it until just a moment ago." She leaned over, looking skyward through the café window. "Who created these?"

"*Mi vara ayleh?*"

"What?"

"*Mi vara ayleh?* It's Hebrew for 'Who created these?' It's from Isaiah 40:26."

"You could recognize it, just like that?"

"It's a very well-known verse. It's also something you have in common with the author of the Zohar."

"The Zohar?"

"An important Kabbalistic text. Thirteenth-century Castile."

"And it uses *that* verse?"

"Yes. The author makes it the linchpin for his whole introduction. He looks up to the sky, to what he calls 'the place toward which all eyes gaze,' and asks, 'Who created these?' Just like you did."

"You make me sound so literate."

"Well, you are. Unfortunately, his answer also makes everyone feel like Lou Costello."

"Lou Costello!? How?"

"The author of the Zohar answers his question by saying that when you gaze up to that place and ask, 'Who created these?' then you will discover that 'Who created these.' "

"Who is it?" said Isabel.

"You bought it! The answer is: 'Yes.' "

" 'Yes'? I don't get it."

"The answer is, 'Who.' 'Who created these?' the author claims is not a question; it's a statement: 'Who is the name of the One who created these.' "

"Oh, that's marvelous, simply marvelous." Isabel laughed out loud. "I get it: 'Who's on first?' "

"Bingo! But the Zohar adds something else. It seems to me that the Zohar is also saying that the answer is *the person* who is wise enough to ask, '*Who?*' "

Isabel smiled like a little girl who had just learned to read her first words. To Kalman, she looked very interested and hopefully willing to keep on teaching him more about cosmology.

"Rabbi Zalman Schachter-Shalomi, a contemporary spiritual master, says that the goal of studying Zohar is to make the mind labile."

"Well, it's working. . . ."

The waiter began collecting and conspicuously clanking together the little metal cream pitchers from the tables.

"Kalman?" Isabel said as they walked out onto the street, "what are you doing three weeks from this Saturday morning?"

"It's *Shabbos*, I usually go to services."

"Perhaps you'd like to go to a bar mitzvah with me?"

"Sure," he said, "just as long as you promise not to tell anyone I'm a rabbi."

ANDALUCÍA

In the same year that Columbus (who some suspect may himself have been a secret Jew) set sail from Palos for a new route to the East, Ferdinand and Isabella succumbed to the pressures of the Inquisition and signed a decree expelling the Jews from

Spain. It was a cataclysm of staggering proportions. With a signature, centuries of Spanish Jewish civilization were abolished. Buildings looted, fortunes lost, families scattered, libraries vanished.

In one of the hundreds of boats that summer leaving the port of Palos for Tangiers was an old man whose life had been devoted to maintaining the synagogue and its adjoining academy in Valladolid. The community employed him to summon the congregation at the set times for prayer, supervise the synagogue, maintain its library, and serve as a community secretary. Like every other Jew in that horrific year, he also had to make painful choices; many precious things would have to be left behind. After his personal possessions, he arranged for a dozen men to each take one volume of different tractates of the Talmud. He himself would carry the folios of the Zohar.

The sea and the sky that morning were both bright azure; it was hard to tell where one ended and the other began. There was hardly any wind. The sails filled, then luffed, then filled again. The old man stood on the swaying deck, watching the Iberian Peninsula disappear, when he became aware of a little boy, no more than seven or eight years old, who was kneeling at his side. Too short to see over the rail, he was peering through a hawsehole.

"Where are your parents, young man?"

The boy pointed toward the crowd of passengers pressed together up at the bow, all squinting into the same nameless future.

"Have you ever seen the ocean before?"

"No, but it must be very, very deep."

"I am sure it is," said the old man.

"Do you think Leviathan lives down there?"

"I am sure he does."

"You know, if God wanted him to, Leviathan could swallow this whole boat in one mouthful." He opened his little mouth as wide as he could in demonstration.

The old man put his hand on the boy's shoulder. "But he will not."

"How do *you* know?"

"Because even Leviathan works for God."

The boy reflected for a moment on this new and comforting piece of theology, and then, eyeing the old man's bundle leaning against the rail: "What is in there?"

"They are some manuscripts I take care of."

"What are they about?"

"Oh, about the mysteries of life."

Then, after some more reflection: "I can read, you know."

"Really? Is that so? Can you read this?" The old man reached into one of the bags and carefully unwrapped a stitched bundle of pages from one of the volumes of Zohar. He pointed to a phrase.

The boy cautiously sounded out each syllable: "*Bo-tzee-na . . . d'Qar-di-nu-ta . . .* What does it mean?" His eyes reflected the sunlight on the waves.

"It means, I believe, that there are things in the heavens above and in the waters beneath that people will never understand."

"You mean like Leviathan?"

"Yes." The old man smiled. "Like Leviathan."

Three

MANHATTAN

Technology may have taken enormous strides in the last 500 years, but for about the last 490 of them the glue business has not changed one bit. The glue they use to stick sheets of paper together to make the cardboard of book covers, for instance, is essentially the same wheat paste you used in kindergarten. Take some flour, mix it with water, and heat it. If you want to get fancy, you can add a pinch of sugar. It's that simple. The resulting gelatinous broth, however, is not simple. It's a highly complex protein molecule, or enzyme, that can be produced only by living cells. The molecules create what chemists call an alpha-glucosidic chemical bond; they attach themselves—like little keys inserted into keyholes that are then turned ninety degrees so that they cannot be removed. It works so well, is so inexpensive to make, and is so simple to use that no one has bothered trying to improve on it. Successive waves of heating and cooling over decades and centuries, however, eventually can create what chemists call "embrittlement," which is just another way of saying that the little keys gradually turn back ninety degrees and fall out of their respective keyholes. It's as if ten thousand keys suddenly turned in ten thousand locks. And that was how the page glued inside the back cover of Kalman's Zohar was released.

Kalman was grading papers in his study when the phone rang. It was Wasserhardt.

"I was right!" Alex whispered as if someone might be eavesdropping. "Rivkin says it's definitely fourteenth century. There is no question."

"How could he know for sure?" Reflexively, Kalman whispered back.

"It was in one of his catalogs; he found the watermark! Remember how we thought it was a horse? Well, it's not a horse; it's a unicorn."

"A unicorn?"

"*Jah*, a unicorn. That's how he knows. And the shop that used the unicorn watermark only made their paper at the very beginning of the fourteenth century."

"That's incredible."

"I didn't believe it, either, but then he showed me the pages from the catalog that indexes all the watermarks. And right there, sure enough, was the unicorn."

"Did he say anything else?"

"He said your guy is from Guadalajara."

"Guadalajara?"

"That's what the 'd'Vadi al-Hajra' in his signature means, Guadalajara."

"No way. That's where Moshe de Leon was from, Guadalajara. Are you thinking what I'm thinking?"

"Well, Rivkin also said that Mr. Moshe from Guadalajara was a Kabbalist."

"Rivkin knows Kabbalah, too?"

"Oh yes. The man who lived next door to him when he was a kid took him under his wing. In fact, Rivkin told me that when he escaped from the Nazis on his way to Treblinka, the guy next to him on the transport was a *m'kubal*, a Kabbalist, too."

"Some train ride."

"Do you believe it? On his way to hell, he winds up sitting next to a Kabbalist! Rivkin said the Kabbalist told him that *botzina d'quardinuta* and *alma d'ah-tay*—the phrases in *your* page—were the Zohar's answer to the *raza d'razin*—the secret of secrets. He had asked the Kabbalist: 'If God is already everything, then why bother making all these separate pieces that don't fit together?' And the man told him: '*Botzina d'qardinuta*—a spark of darkness—and *alma d'ah-tay*—the world to come. Don't ever forget.'"

"How old did you say Rivkin was?"

"Eighty-one, maybe eighty-two. Why?"

"I guess he never forgot. Did he say anything about that spot at the top where you said it looks like something might have been erased?"

"He said, 'Oxford.'"

"Oxford?"

"He sent it to a friend at Oxford who does ultraviolet photography."

"He had to send it all the way to England?"

"Rivkin has an old friend there he trusts. Don't worry; it will be safe. You must be patient, Kalman. These things, they take time."

"Well, it's already waited several centuries; I suppose it could stand a few more weeks."

Kalman hung up and removed a folded photocopy of the page from his jacket pocket. Then, after examining it again, he taped it above his desk. He pronounced each of its words carefully, as if they were an incantation. Nothing happened. Then he spoke to the page: "Just what are you doing in a book with my name on it?" It did not answer. "I may never have had a mystical experience, but you are something equally precious and more important. You have come down through the generations *for me.* . . ."

CASTILE

The author of the Zohar should be an inspiration to writers of historical fiction. Here was a man who actually pulled it off. He imagined himself back into second-century Palestine. Relying solely on accounts from the Talmud, he created the people, customs, and geography. He even invented his own version of Palestinian Aramaic. But this does not mean it was necessarily a hoax. Many important religious works have likewise been composed pseudepigraphically.

Scholem reminds us that such claims of ancient authorship are often the writer's attempt to subjugate his own desire for fame. Or perhaps the author simply could not imagine he could write something so luminous and sincerely believed he was the channeled instrument of a long-dead sage. But whatever the motive, the Zohar's authorship remains a continuing mystery to the present day. No less a scholar than the contemporary Polish mystic Aaron Zeitman was convinced of the Zohar's antiquity.

The first time the five-foot-one-inch Castilian acrobat saw Don Judah's library, he froze in the doorway—afraid to enter, unable to leave. Here, before him in this room, this shrine, were more scrolls and sheaves of pages than there were even in the academy at the synagogue in Barcelona! Even a preliminary stroll past a few of the shelves confirmed that, while many of the books were in Greek, Latin, Spanish, French, and Arabic, a great many were also in Hebrew. Moshe was spellbound.

"Don Moshe ben Shem Tov, señora," he said as Don Judah's wife entered. "I am at your service."

"You are . . . shorter than I expected—and more . . ." She fumbled for a tactful word. "Muscular."

"You were perhaps expecting someone frail?"

"I had imagined that a scholar of your repute . . ."

"This library is amazing, señora. There are several books here I should very much like to read."

"My husband, Don Judah, collects them," she said. "He only

knows the rudiments of Hebrew, but he does so love his books. Only last month he bought a whole crateful of scrolls from a Turk—after simply opening the lid." She walked over to one of the shelves, removed a sheaf of pages, and opened it. "Here," she said to her new teacher, "would you like to hear me read? I have learned the letters myself." And, sounding out each syllable: "*Sha-ah-rey Oh-rah.*"

"Bravo! Well done. It means Gates of Light. In Toledo you learned to read like that? Can you read the next line also?"

"*Yo-sef Gik-a . . . Gik-a . . .*"

"Yosef Gikatilla."

"Yes, Yosef Gikatilla, that's it."

"He is the author."

"How did you know?"

"He is my friend."

"What is he like?"

"He is a rotund philosopher who likes to imagine he's a Kabbalist."

"You say that as if it were a defect."

Moshe smiled. "Only if you try to have an argument with him."

"I am certain that my husband, Judah, would love to meet him. He is fascinated by authors. Do you think that you could arrange it?"

"Easily. I would like to meet your husband again, too. I only spoke with him for a short time when he hired me. He seemed very busy. But he never asked me about my Hebrew, and he seemed almost relieved by my height. Why would he care that I am short?"

"You may have noticed that he has insisted that when we

meet my maid must always be present." She nodded to the woman standing discreetly in the corner. Moshe bowed again.

"It sounds like your husband loves you very much."

"My husband loves to surround himself with wisdom, with books, with beautiful things." She looked away, avoiding his glance. Then she said, "He believes that beautiful possessions are the measure of a man. . . ."

Tuesday has always been propitious among the Jews. That is the day in the biblical creation sequence about which God said, "It was good," not once, but twice. And so each week, on that day also, during the hot summers, the señora's driver would place two chairs and a small table in one of the fields near Valladolid for his mistress and her Hebrew tutor. Sometimes she would instruct her maid to bring oranges, figs, and sweet wine.

"Tell me again, Don Moshe, about what the midrash says about the light that is hidden throughout creation. It has been in my thoughts all week. What did you call it, again? *Or ganooz*—hidden light?"

"Yes, *or ganooz*; that is correct, señora. If you think about it, you can deduce almost everything from the biblical story itself. It is a very important principle of midrash: Everything is already there, present *in the text*—everything. It is simply not apparent on a casual first reading. Tell me: What did God make on day one?"

She thought for a moment. "Evening and morning?"

"No, no, no. Those were only the *result*. What did *God* make? Remember, God creates through speaking."

"Oh, of course, light? Yes, that's it. The first thing was light. God said, 'Let there be light!' " Her face brightened.

"Very good. Now, can you tell me, on what day did God make the sun, the moon—all the heavenly lights?"

"I don't know. Was it day four?"

"Excellent! You may seat yourself in the row of the best students in the class."

She laughed. "But I am already in the front row." Then, looking around for effect: "And I am also in the back row."

"Well, then, señora, if God did not make the heavenly lights until day four, would you please tell me what is the problem?"

"From where did the light of day one come?"

"Exactly, from where *did* it come?"

"I do not know. I never considered it before. Don Moshe, there must be some *other* kind of light."

"Correct. It was knowing-light, the light of wisdom. According to one midrash," said Moshe, "that light of the first day was seventy times brighter than the sun! It was so brilliant that when Adam and Eve were created on day six, they never even noticed the sun! The light was so bright that, in its radiance, they could see from one end of creation to the other end of time."

"That means, then, that they could see us sitting here now!" The señora thought for a minute and then waved toward the sky. "Adam, can you hear me? You must listen carefully to what I am about to say. It is very important. Very soon Eve is going to offer you a piece of fruit. You must *not* eat of it. Do you hear me? If you do, it will commence a chain of terrible events!" Her maid looked up from her sewing.

"But remember," replied her tutor, "then there would be no

history. No Jerusalem. No Babylonia. No Castile. No oranges. No donkey cart. You and I would never be."

She thought again and announced to the sky: "Adam, if you are still listening, I did not mean the words I spoke only moments ago. Go right ahead; eat of the fruit. Enjoy it! My God," she said, "with that light, the two of them would know *everything*, would they not? *Nothing* would be concealed from them. But wait, I do not understand." She looked up into the high clouds. "If they could see the future, then why did they eat the fruit? . . . Unless, by eating of it, they were deliberately saying, 'We would rather *not* be able to see the future. We prefer to die ignorant of the future than to live forever!' They are both of one piece, Don Moshe, are they not? Knowledge *and* immortality, good *and* evil, life *and* death. Is it not possible that this is what God intended all along?"

Don Moshe ben Shem Tov de Guadalajara stared at her. He had no category for such a student. "Please, señora," he said, fumbling with the bottle and his quill, "one more moment, please, while I open the ink. . . . Yes, thank you. Now please speak those words again, but I beseech you, señora, this time, slower."

Over the next few summers, this teacher-student relationship—at least when it came to intuiting the nature of divine reality—evolved toward symmetry. Each year King Alfonso the Wise would move his household to Valladolid, and his courtiers would move with him. And each summer Moshe would teach his gifted student Hebrew and Aramaic seasoned with Kabbalah, and she would teach him about the mystery of existence and other matters for which humanity only rarely seems able to find the proper words.

"Some people," he once confided to his friend Yosef, "it is as if they have been alive for ten thousand years. She is an *old* soul. She knows the answer to questions before I can finish asking them." And that was how it went. She could not learn Hebrew and Aramaic fast enough; he could not record her words fast enough. Once he said, "How can you know that? It's as if you're reading words written in the shape of the clouds. What you said last week, señora, it sounds exactly as if it is from Midrash Genesis Rabba, but it is not written in exactly those words. You have added something else."

She shrugged. "The words come into my head and I say them."

"Well, they are also in the midrash. Are you sure you have never read it before? What you said about hiding light is exquisite. Here, listen. Since we last met I have located the passage in the midrash, and then I rewrote your words:

> The light the Holy One created during the work of creation shone from one end of space to the other end of time, but then it was hidden away. And why? So the wicked of the world wouldn't be able to use it or despoil countless worlds.

"You make me sound so very wise."

"Oh no, señora, they are really your ideas, I have only rewritten them."

"But I still do not understand, Don Moshe," she said. "Why did not God just extinguish the light? Why did God then have to go to all the trouble of hiding it?"

"That one I believe I *can* answer. Think for a moment: What is the alternative? If God were to remove even the *possibility* of that ultimate knowing, it would *also* destroy creation. A universe with no chance of awareness, no self-reflection, is also void of even the possibility of redemption. Creation would be futile, pointless, a waste."

"Of course," she said. "And the only place big enough to hide the light of awareness is inside *all* creation. The big light is hidden—within *everything!* Not just in the Torah scroll or in the prayers or in the flowers, but in rocks and in dirt and in the donkey and, yes, I suppose, even in death. If you are righteous, you can find it everywhere."

A flock of geese in formation, signaling the end of summer, flew overhead. Following them for a moment, she said, "You can read it everywhere. Nothing is beneath being a vessel for the light. It is planted like a seed for the righteous."

Moshe realized he was looking not at the geese, but at his student. He dipped his quill into the ink again. "Slower, please. Let me write this before I forget your words: 'Light . . . is sown . . . for the righteous. . . .' It is so beautiful. But wait, I have heard that before. 'Light is sown for the righteous.' It is from the Book of Psalms. You were quoting the Bible."

"Was I?"

"You did not realize it?"

"I have read only a few of King David's psalms, but it does seem obvious to me that such a light, hidden away, could nourish creation. I mean, the mere fact of its existence, even though it be hidden, is sufficient."

Moshe nodded. Of course, now it was obvious to him also.
Then he wrote:

Through that light, the world endures. Every single day a
ray issues from that hidden light and sustains the entire
world; through it, the Holy One nourishes creation.

INTRODUCTION TO *THE BOOK OF LOVE*

Kalman hung his jacket on a hook on the back of his office
door and sat down at his desk. Off to one side was a pile of
mail, periodicals, and interoffice memos that had been growing
on the desktop like mushrooms after a rainstorm. It was near
the bottom of the stack that he found a photocopied article
from the *Chicago Review of Hermeneutical Studies* entitled "Some
Fragments from *Sefer Ahavah, The Book of Love*, Salonika, *Circa*
1603, Assembled with an Introduction and Critical Apparatus
by M. Eisenbogen." The article itself was dated September
1930. Clipped to its half-dozen fine-print pages was a library
call slip with a very neatly #3-penciled note: "Kalman, I think
you should read this one. —Alex."

"Huh," Kalman said to himself, unsure of what to expect.
Wasserhardt did occasionally send him photocopies, but their
accompanying notes never had such specific instructions. So
he leaned back in his chair, propped his feet up on the desk,
and read the article.

Sefer Ahavah, The Book of Love, has been lost; its author is unknown. . . .

Kalman sang, "Dum, dum, dum, dum . . . Who wrote *The Book of Love?*" and laughed out loud. "Oh, Alex, Alex, if you only knew American pop music."

Our knowledge of its existence comes from allusions to it in other texts referring to the title and city of its publication. Unfortunately, only a handful of sections of the text remain. From what has survived, however, we can conclude that *The Book of Love* was a commentary on Song of Songs. Long a favorite of mystics—orgasm and mystic union both share the ecstasy of losing the boundaries of self—Song of Songs is understood not as an anthology of pastoral love poetry, but as an allegory of the romance between Israel and God.

Perhaps the most fascinating passage is launched by a simple pun on the Hebrew of Songs 1:3, "The maidens (*alamot*) love you." The plain meaning of the word *alamot* is maidens. But with only a subtle shift in pronunciation, the word can also be deliberately (mis)read as *olamot*— worlds. "Therefore do *worlds* love you"—one after another, a loving that transcends lifetimes and generations. . . .

"What the . . . ?" said Kalman, looking back to the first page for the details of the article's publication. It was not a joke. He had heard of the *Chicago Review*; it was, indeed, a respected journal. Removing a red pen from the mug of pens on his desk, he underlined the last phrase: "a loving that transcends lifetimes and generations." The phone rang, but Kalman did not pick it up.

With this simple pun on "worlds" and "maidens," the anonymous author of *The Book of Love* proposes a novel theory of life after death. Most theories are but transparent attempts to soften the sting of mortality. They all say, in effect, "I love myself so much, I cannot imagine I will ever end." Common examples include transmigration of souls, ghosts, and reincarnation. . . .

Kalman remembered how Slomovitz had, years ago, ruined this one for him: "Doesn't it strike you as odd, old boy, that of all the tens of thousands of people who claim to have been reincarnated from past lives, not one single one of them ever told anyone where he hid the money?"

The Book of Love proposes another model. This theory, however, offers no emotional comfort—which is doubtless the principal reason for its obscurity. While proposing the existence of translifetime memory, the theory does so at the expense of identity. Consciousness survives, our text claims, but identity, alas, does not! Upon dying, you must, as it were, surrender your passport. To be sure, what you knew and experienced may survive you, but *you* won't know it. Someone else, however, centuries later might. . . .

As he turned the page, Kalman caught sight of his wristwatch: "Ieyaah!" He sprang out of the chair. "Seven minutes late already!" If he sprinted, he knew he could make it to class in under four minutes. And if he could make it there before anyone left, a major embarrassment might yet be averted. He grabbed his papers and text and ran.

POLAND

"My name is Aaron Zeitman."

"Aaron Zeitman?" The young man looked at him in disbelief.

"I doubt that there is more than one—and if there were another, I wish I—"

The screech of the train's brakes stopped him in midsentence.

"I am sorry; I did not hear what you just said."

"I wish I were he."

"Who?"

"No one. It's not important. I wish I were someone who was somewhere else."

"But you are Aaron Zeitman?"

"Yes. I am he."

"I read your article 'On the Border of Two Worlds'—the one where you claim that Judaism is mystical and not rational and conclude that Moshe de Leon was only the final redactor of the Zohar but *not* its author. Brilliant!"

The older man unconsciously smoothed his beard. "Thank you; I'm honored. Only a few people have read it, and most of them were not nearly as generous in their reactions. Wherever did you find it?"

"The man who lived next door to us was a Kabbalist. Even though I was too young, he secretly took me under his wing. He had no children of his own. . . ."

Zeitman nodded. "The Zohar is simply more than one person could've written. There is no way Moshe de Leon could've done it all himself." He glanced over at the woman leaning against his interlocutor. "I think she is dead," he whispered. "She has not moved for several hours. And look"—he motioned toward his own mouth as he exhaled a small puff of vapor in the cold winter air—"I cannot see her breath."

Together they watched her mouth. Finally, the young man reached over and held his fingertips to the side of the woman's neck, seeking a nonexistent pulse. Then he shook her gently, but there was no response.

Zeitman shook his head and whispered, "Blessed be the One who is indeed the Judge." And the young man respectfully eased the woman's lifeless body from his shoulder and onto the floor. He removed her coat and covered her face.

Together the two men surveyed the gaunt faces of the other passengers in the boxcar. They remained silent for some time. Then Zeitman said, "Where did you learn Zohar?"

"My neighbor. His whole family—father, grandfather, great-grandfather, as far back as anyone knows—Kabbalists, every one. He wasn't supposed to tell the secrets to someone my age, but when he realized that there would be no one to teach, well, you know, he was a teacher; he had to give it to someone. One evening he said to me, 'Dovid, you are meant for the Zohar.' "

" 'Meant for the Zohar'?"

"I think it was his way of saying that I had a knack for understanding it."

The older man's face brightened. "I'm sorry, I didn't catch your name."

"Dovid."

"It's a pleasure to meet you, Dovid. . . ."

"Dovid Rivkin."

"Herr Rivkin."

"Do you mind if I ask you a question, Professor?"

Zeitman smiled.

"Well, I'm sure you have noticed that the God described in the Zohar also has a feminine side. What I want to know is, where does that idea come from? I mean, all of a sudden, in this book, God is also a woman. That is surprising to me."

"Perhaps," he replied, "the author of the Zohar was drawing on other sources. You know, sources that were more feminine. Women know things we do not. They can give birth. . . ."

MANHATTAN

Alone in the taxi, after Kalman had walked her through the sequence of how to dress a scroll of the Torah, Isabel Benveniste realized she kept picturing the rabbi's hands. Then she surprised herself by laughing out loud as she recalled his joke about the rabbit in Minnesota. On one side of the equation, the rabbi obviously found her interesting. He was literate and engaging. On the other side, he was overweight and disorganized. And then there was the way he spoke when he got excited. He might make an interesting companion at difficult dinner parties, but nothing more.

But when he called in less than a week, inviting her to join him for a one-night showing of Krzysztof Kieslowski's film *Red*, she surprised herself by saying, "Why, yes, I'd love to."

She enjoyed the film and was engaged by its themes of privacy and the interconnectedness of lives. The final scene seemed to say that, one way or another, you find whom you're supposed to find.

"Kalman," Isabel said later that evening as they walked over to a coffee shop, "I'm curious about the way . . ."

"I speak sometimes?" he said.

"Well, yes. Every now and then, your syntax seems too . . ."

"I apologize. I should have told you sooner. It started when I was in ninth grade. And after a few difficult experiences, I just got used to it. You know how it is, you invent little workarounds. And when I have to give a speech, I write it out in advance."

"And other times?"

"You mean socially? If I'm real nervous, it's harder."

"You don't have any trouble talking to me."

"It's called dysnomia. Some visiting speech pathologist in high school gave me a name for it. Basically, when I'm under a lot of pressure or very excited, I can't always find the right words in time and my syntax gets screwed up. The doctor told me that it might go away all by itself, but just in case, I should make friends with it."

"Didn't Moses also have trouble speaking—stuttering or something?"

"You've been holding out on me, Benveniste."

"I may not be religious, but I am literate in Western civilization."

"It's in Exodus. It says that Moses was *aral s'fatayim*—literally, 'of uncircumcised lips.' "

"That sounds like enough to make any man stutter."

"No, really, that is exactly what the Hebrew says. Unfortunately, nobody knows for sure what it means."

"I always thought it meant he was a stammerer."

"That is certainly one reasonable and common interpretation. But the precise sense of the original Hebrew idiom has been lost. There are a whole slew of traditions about how holy men have speech impediments. According to the midrash, the—"

"Midrash?"

"Not commentary, but stories woven in and out of biblical stories. A good midrash will not elucidate the meaning of the biblical text but will be much more likely to forever ruin it. Here's a good example. As a child, according to one midrash, Abraham tried to eat a glowing coal and injured his tongue. The Bible itself says that the prophet Isaiah also had his mouth consecrated to speak God's word when it was touched with a red hot ember. My own hunch is that it's the same motif with Moses's speech: The greatest prophet of them all, the greatest instrument for the Divine Voice, also has a damaged mouth. Martin Buber, the philosopher, says that the tragedy of revelation is that it is 'laid upon the stammering to bring the voice of Heaven to Earth.' "

Isabel contemplated Kalman's lips as he spoke. They looked perfectly normal to her.

"Isabel, may I ask *you* a personal question?"

"It is only fair."

"Well, I'm wondering, an attractive, accomplished woman like yourself, how come you . . ."

"Live alone?" she said, completing the hard part.

Kalman nodded. Her answer was polished, perhaps just a bit too rehearsed.

"I seriously considered marriage twice," she said. "Both times in my early thirties. But when we got close to making an announcement, I suppose you could say that caution won out over romance."

"But caution won't keep you warm on a cold winter night."

"That might be understood as either a proposition or a proposal," she said with a smile.

Kalman's mouth went dry. (*Quick, for God's sake, tell her she is good-looking! But I already said she was attractive. It doesn't matter, say it again.*)

"Mean . . . I . . . very attractive . . . Please . . . do not misunder . . . understand. . . . My therapist . . . my therapist says I . . . away . . . afraid of giving myself . . . away."

He could not tell what was behind her smile or whether he had offended her or hurt her or, for that matter, right now, even what exactly was going on.

"And you?"

"I was married for two and a half years," said Kalman, regaining some composure. "Let's just say it was not a good idea."

She understood, from how he spoke it, that there had been a wound and that it had still not healed and that any further questions, right now, would probably be unwelcome.

"Here," he said, hoping to change the topic. He reached inside his jacket and removed the photocopy. "I think I may have stumbled upon something really fascinating and maybe important, too."

It was a handwritten paragraph of Aramaic. Below that was what appeared to be its translation. Isabel saw that it was signed by someone named Moshe ben Shem Tov de Guadalajara.

"Who is Moshe ben Shem Tov de Guadalajara?"

"Thirteenth-, fourteenth-century Spain. There's an outside chance that he might be the same as Moshe ben Shem Tov de Leon who wrote the Zohar, easily the most important work of Kabbalah ever written." (That was the first time he had ever said it out loud to anyone.)

Isabel looked more closely at the photocopy. "That sounds very impressive, Kalman, but I don't understand why you are showing me . . . ?"

SAFED: THIRD ITERATION

Kalman nodded; the old man nodded back. There were only the two of them there, and Kalman felt a little awkward. So he said, "I'm a rabbi from the United States; I'm leading a tour."

The old man nodded again. "The afternoon service doesn't start for an hour yet."

"Thank you. Are you the *shammas* here?"

He shook his head.

"I just thought, since you were sweeping the floor like that . . ."

"No."

"May I ask who you are?" Kalman said.

"Oh, I'm just someone who tries to see to it that what's *supposed* to happen happens."

"I beg your pardon?"

"It's not something you could point to."

"Try me."

"Oh, just . . . helping people notice what they're supposed to notice, two people meeting one another, things like that."

"What are you saying?"

"I try to help people find what they're supposed to find. You know, the astronomy lecture."

"The astronomy lecture!? I don't understand. What are you talking about?"

"I try to help people find each other."

"But what if I wasn't interested in cosmology or she didn't have that bar mitzvah invitation?"

"Then that would be a miss."

"A miss?"

"Yes, a miss. Haven't you ever looked back over the years and realized that something or someone who is now terribly important to you had crossed your path before but, at the time, you missed it? You say, 'My God, we must've *both* been in the *same* room twenty years ago, but we never met'?"

"Sure, everybody has."

"Well, that was a miss."

"That would mean, then, that life is mainly filled with misses."

"This surprises you?"

"No, now that you put it that way. And what's a hit?"

"That's when what is supposed to happen, finally happens."

"And they lived happily ever after."

"Who said anything about happiness?"

"But sooner or later people get what's coming to them?"

"No, I'm sorry, but it's not about reward or punishment."

"Then, bad things just happen?"

"Mazel tov! For that, you don't need theology. No, people receive countless opportunities to be reverent before whatever is set before them. Sometimes it's a wedding, sometimes a funeral. It could be a sunny spring morning; it could be a cancer ward. You don't get to choose the event. You only get to choose whether or not you will be reverent."

"And if you choose reverence?"

"Oh, then you're guaranteed the fulfillment that can only come from realizing you're doing exactly what you're *supposed* to be doing in precisely that place and at precisely that moment."

"Even if your situation is miserable?"

"Even if you're living in a sewer, racked with pain, and on the brink of death. But you already know that—everyone does. There are no guarantees of happiness. The closest, I guess, you can come to happiness is the elusive satisfaction of knowing you're doing what has been set before you to accomplish."

"What about if what you're doing is wrong or evil?"

"You ever try to be reverent *and* injure someone at the same time? Sorry, it can't be done."

"Then being reverent leads you to be good?"

"No, just grateful to be able to do the next thing, and that *usually*, but not always, leads to being good."

"Why wouldn't everyone be reverent, then, all the time?"

The old man thought for a minute. "Because you—and just about everybody else—get to thinking that you are in charge. You imagine you can run things all by yourselves. You get carried away and start imagining you're autonomous and have free will and that you're really running your own lives. You know. You get to thinking you are like God. And the minute that happens, you stop being reverent. What got you to pick up this old Zohar, for instance? Was it really free will? Why'd you split off from your tour group this afternoon?"

He reached up to a bookcase, brought down tractate *Berakhot* of the Talmud, and, without even looking, opened it to folio 33b. He pointed to the words in the middle of the page, but from the direction of his gaze, it seemed as if he were reading from what was written on the ceiling: " 'Everything's in the hands of Heaven except for one thing: Whether or not you're reverent.' That part's up to you. That's the only expression of your free will."

MANHATTAN

Vertical cities became feasible in 1854, when a Vermont machinist named Elisha Graves Otis demonstrated the first safety hoister. Until then, objects being lifted by a rope were only as safe as the strength of the rope. Otis's invention employed a heavy steel wagon spring with a ratchet and pawls preventing the platform from falling. Under the management of P. T. Barnum himself, at New York City's Crystal Palace Exposition, to the horror of onlookers, Otis had himself raised to a height of forty feet, whereupon an assistant with an ax severed the rope! Viewers gasped as the platform remained in place. Otis swept off his top hat, bowed, and proclaimed, "All safe, gentlemen, all safe!"

Even though he knew they were safe, Kalman still did not like elevators. He disliked tight spaces—crowded subways, buses, and especially elevators. Over the years, he had learned to insulate himself from these inescapable confinements of city life by closing his eyes and breathing slowly. But, given not too much vertical distance, he chose the stairwell instead. As fate would have it, however, Isabel's condominium was on the thirty-second floor.

On his first visit there, Kalman walked quickly over to Isabel's living room window and stood there, taking several deep breaths. It was a Sunday afternoon in November. Without diverting his gaze from the expansive view, he said, "Have you ever been to the top?"

"Of what?" Isabel said, walking out of the hallway behind him.

"The Chrysler Building. Have you ever been to the top?" He turned around to face her.

"I have never even been in the lobby. I must have been on the corner of Lex and Forty-second a thousand times, but, you know, I never once thought to walk inside."

"Me neither."

"Did you know there was some kind of skyscraper race and that for a short time the Chrysler was the tallest building in the world?"

"How do you know *that*?"

"I read it somewhere. My memory snags stray facts." As she moved her head, he watched a curl of hair jiggle in front of each ear.

"A few more curls," said Kalman, "and you'd have a pair of *payos* that would make any Hasid proud."

"You mean like the Jews in black hats?" She took her right index finger and wound one lock of black hair around it. "Like this?"

"*Libay-tini b'ahat may-ae-naiykh.*"

"What?"

"It's from the Bible. It means 'You have stolen my heart with one glance,'" said Kalman.

"It sounds so romantic in the Hebrew, so . . . holy. They are related, holiness and romance, yes?"

He looked at her. What an extraordinary mind.

"Here," said Isabel, "I have something I think you'll want to see." She gestured toward a small sofa behind the coffee table. She sat beside him, placing a large folio on the table. "It's the pictures I promised to show you, not the sort of thing you might find at your local bookstore. They are computer-enhanced photos of the cosmic microwave background that have come in from a new satellite. . . ."

"Why, Professor Benveniste, I do believe you have lured me up here to show me your galaxies."

He thought it was only a joke; she hoped he would go on thinking it was.

Together they turned the pages.

"Isabel," he said, "I know you can't see these things through a telescope. What . . . I mean, how do you do it?"

She turned to face him. "There are three ways to do cosmology. One is theoretical. You start from basic laws of physics and then apply them to the universe. If you're very fortunate, sometimes you might even find that they don't work the way they're supposed to."

"That's fortunate?"

"Oh, yes. It means that some basic theory is wrong, and that can initiate a minor revolution in scientific thought. It's the stuff of Nobel Prizes. You try to come up with equations that could explain how the universe began. Then there are what I call number crunchers. These are the guys who do numerical simulations. You see, very often the equations the theories generate are themselves just so complex that only a computer can solve them. So what the number crunchers do is postulate a series of givens, feed it all into the machine, and watch how the model itself plays out."

"Alone in a room with a computer terminal."

"Yes."

"No telescopes?"

"No telescopes. Don't look so sad, Kal. There's a third group. Scientists, like me, still do cosmology the old-fashioned way, by observing things."

"But how?"

"Obviously we can't use optical telescopes. They can't see far enough, and our eyes can't register the kinds of data we need. So we use a CCD, a charge-coupled device—it's basically the same technology they're using in those new digital cameras, only it's a lot more precise and a whole lot more expensive. We are able to record detailed images of what the universe looked like one hundred thousand years after the big bang and study the basic structures in the universe itself—the distribution and movement of galaxies. Here, for example . . ."

She flipped through several pages of magenta, purple, and red oval plates that looked like something one might have picked up in the gift shop at the MoMA or the Whitney.

"You're telling me that these are images of the past?"

"Remember, the farther away—"

"Yes, I know. The farther away in space, the farther away in time."

"Excellent student! And then, through spectral photography we are also able to identify the chemical composition of a distant light source."

"How?"

"Every element has its own spectral signature. For instance, if you run an electrical current through neon gas, it will glow red and red orange. Here, look at these. . . ."

With each new image, his eyes widened more. "Unbelievable," he whispered. He turned to face her. "Thank you."

"I hoped you would like it."

"Like it? I love it." He leaned back on the sofa, clasping his hands behind his head. "When I was in the ninth grade, I had a science teacher who was a big astronomy nut. At the time, I didn't have the vocabulary to get my head around much of it, but something happened during a field trip. Our class had all assembled in this observatory on the roof of a Harvard building, and I remember that I lost track of time. There was some kind of box. It had three buttons that controlled the rotation of the observatory's dome and its big slit for the telescope. Mr. Smolens—that was his name—pressed the third button. I remember that. And, presto, the roof opened. It took me by complete surprise. Roofs aren't supposed to open. But it wasn't just the slit in the roof that opened. As I reflect back, it was as if the button also controlled a window in my brain."

"Kalman, I had no idea . . ."

Kalman was startled, both by how much of himself he had inadvertently just given her and, even more, by how easy it was to do so. Such openness, however, made him feel anxious—as if he were in a crowded elevator.

That evening, on her way to bed, Isabel walked into the living room to shut off the lights. She looked at the open book of galaxies, as Kalman had poetically called it, lying on the coffee table. Then she walked over to the window and looked at the spire of the Chrysler Building just as he had. She watched a helicopter with its flashing lights move in slow motion over the city. She surveyed the grid of midtown Manhattan streets below: red taillights on Second going downtown and, on Third, white headlights heading uptown; taillights along Forty-seventh running west over to the Hudson and (even though it was out of her line of sight) headlights on Forty-eighth running toward the East River. For a moment, she imagined that this orthogonal pattern had not been devised by city planners, but instead was the expression of some underlying cosmic design. And anyone—with sufficient organization and patience—could eventually understand everything that existed. Everything, that is, except this stammering rabbi she'd picked up in the Village a few weeks ago. And now she'd gone and invited him up to show him photos from the orbital Chandra X-ray Observatory of Cygnus A. Jesus Christ, she might just as well have invited him up to see her etchings!

He was so eager, like a little boy. But then, when they were alone together, he hadn't touched her. He had quoted that phrase from the Song of Songs. But then why hadn't he made some kind of advance? He was afraid. That was it. The man was obviously afraid. But what was he afraid of? He didn't want to talk about his marriage. He must have been very hurt. Maybe she had died tragically.

She stared out the window for a while, trying to understand. With a bare foot, she stepped on the floor switch and the standing lamp obediently turned itself off.

· FOUR ·

BOSTON

This is how Kalman *really* lost his wife: He had returned home from officiating at his cousin's wedding in Evanston to find that all of Elaine's possessions were gone and so was Elaine. The only remaining physical evidence of her presence in his life— she even took the photos from the album!—was a letter placed conspicuously in the middle of the dining room table. It was leaning up against a bouquet of flowers that he had brought her before leaving for the wedding. The letter was, he would later say, mercifully direct and unequivocal. "Now I understand . . . ," she had written, "our marriage could never work." She had fallen in love with her Shakespeare professor. She wanted a divorce so they could get married. She was sincerely sorry that things had turned out like this. And, by the way, she was also touched by the bouquet of flowers. They were beautiful.

And they were still beautiful, even a few days later when they had begun to lose their petals. The brightly colored, delicate little blossom pieces lay there collecting on the wooden table right where they had fallen, wanting nothing other than to be returned to the earth and left alone to decompose.

Over the weeks and months that followed, Kalman's pain turned introspective. Instead of targeting Elaine for inflicting such injury, he concluded that the true source of his grief was love's transience and his own vulnerability to it. "There will always be people out there who will hurt me, and I will have only myself to blame if they succeed," he concluded. "I must make myself like a rock." Yet it was still the same, even months after the divorce: He'd finish off a few glasses of cheap Scotch and fall asleep in the big chair in the living room of the shoebox they had once called home—not toughened one bit, but just as vulnerable as he had always been. And when he woke in the morning and looked into the bathroom mirror, he saw that his eyes were still red.

Then one day, as he walked into the kitchen to make himself some instant coffee, he said, "Enough. If I cannot be a rock, then at least I can pretend I am one."

Kalman marked his decision to return to the world by accepting an invitation from an old classmate to give a talk about his preliminary dissertation work on the twentieth-century Polish mystic Aaron Zeitman. It also meant his first trip out to San Francisco. Out on the coast, he learned that mysticism was hot. Twenty-seven people showed up to hear him talk about Zeitman and the Zohar. A few had even heard of the Zohar.

"Far-out," one colorfully dressed young man, who appeared to be wearing pajamas, remarked during the small reception that followed.

"Kal, it's really important research," said his friend. "I had no idea of the scope of Zeitman's work. You know, I think that there's a book there."

"I'll just be glad if there's one mediocre doctoral thesis."

The day before he was scheduled to return home, another classmate from rabbinic school picked him up for what Kalman thought would be a leisurely drive out into the country. Mordecai (his name used to be Martin, but he had legally changed it to his Hebrew name), it turned out, had bought himself an old VW bus and gotten a modest grant from the local Jewish community federation, and he was ministering to the needs of Jewish flower children who were now having children of their own up in the steep hills in Mendocino and Humboldt counties a few hours north of the city.

"I want to show you the Land," Mordecai said. From the way he had said "the Land," Kalman suspected that it referred not to geography, but to metaphysics. He was glad he had agreed. The Land was indeed more than spectacular; it was breathtaking, awesome.

Their destination was a small settlement in the mountains north of Ukiah, a real, honest-to-goodness hippie commune like the ones Kalman had read about. All the men had beards, none of the women wore brassieres, and as far as he could tell, *everyone* was stoned.

"Don't you have to worry about the police?"

"See that guy over there?" Mordecai gestured toward a

man who was sitting on a big rock, wearing a leather cowboy hat, leather vest, and no shoes, and smoking a joint. "He's the DA."

"I see what you mean."

The topography was very rugged, what a geologist might have described as extreme. There were no naturally flat places. Even more spectacular, a constant onshore Pacific wind, combined with the updrafts from the steep hills, generated an endless stream of puffy, fast-moving clouds. Whenever you looked up, there were scores of them rushing inland, transient gifts from the Pacific.

After lunch and a short tour, Mordecai led him along the top of a steep ridge. Several hundred yards in the distance, he saw that their path led to a white domed structure. From far away, it looked like a very small observatory. As they drew closer, Kalman realized that the dome was made entirely of clear Plexiglas.

"You're gonna love this," Mordecai said.

"Love what? What do I do?"

"You just go inside, Kal. Trust me; you'll figure it out. I'll be back in a while."

Kalman watched Mordecai retrace his steps back down the path along the ridge. The only entrance to the observatory (or whatever it was) was through a door in a small shed attached to one side. It turned out to be a vestibule, big enough for only one person and a bench built into the wall. On the other wall were a few steps and a door leading up into the circular, domed room. The sign on the door read: PLEASE REMOVE YOUR SHOES. (He wondered if its author was deliberately mimicking God's instructions to Moses at the burning bush.) So Kalman obediently removed his shoes. He climbed the stairs and opened the door. There was nothing in the room except plush white wall-to-wall carpeting that extended halfway up the walls. Above that was the clear Plexiglas dome. Through it, Kalman could see the pointed tops of the fir trees and, when he bent backward, above them a sky full of clouds racing inland.

There wasn't anything else to do or see in the room except look at the clouds, so he sat down and looked up. After a few minutes, he concluded that it would be more comfortable to simply lie on his back. He thought about Elaine and what he would preach about next week and if the Red Sox would hire a new manager and the third chapter of *Sefer haTemunah*, which he still couldn't translate, and Aaron Zeitman and about how, in such a place as this, it was natural that Eastern mysticism would find fertile soil and about the ache in his heart. His reverie was interrupted by a soft knock on the door and Mordecai's voice. "Kal? You still in there?"

Kalman sat up to see his friend opening the door. "Hi, Mordecai. You were right; this is really beautiful. Thanks."

"I hoped you'd agree," Mordecai said. "You've been here quite a while."

"Well, when you watch those clouds, time moves by different rules." He put on his shoes.

Mordecai smiled and glanced at his wristwatch. "You know," he said, "you've been here over three hours."

"No way!"

Mordecai held up his watch so that Kalman could see for himself.

"I thought you'd like it."

The two of them were silent as they began walking back along the ridge.

"Mordecai, did you see that Stanley Kubrick movie *2001: A Space Odyssey*?"

"Are you kidding? Everyone in Mendocino County has seen it at least twice. They go for that scene where he slips through the monolith. The sound effects from the audience during that light show are part of the total experience."

Kalman nodded. "Do you remember, near the beginning, there's that gorilla who keeps looking up at the moon?"

"Great scene," said Mordecai. "I figure he was the first religious thinker!"

"And do you know what he was thinking? 'Where did all the time go? I can't believe I'm old enough to have a kid who's getting bar mitzvahed tomorrow.' "

"I think I officiated at that bar mitzvah," said Mordecai.

They both laughed.

"Voilà! The beginning of human culture: It's not learning how to use tools to break heads; culture is humanity's way of trying to mollify the bite of time's passage—I'm too young to be this old."

"How old are you now, Kal?"

"Twenty-eight, Mordi, I'm twenty-eight."

A hawk circled overhead, looking for lunch.

MANHATTAN

Isabel watched as Kalman opened an embroidered blue cloth bag he had placed on the empty pew beside them. He removed a prayer shawl the size of a small tablecloth with black stripes of varying widths along two of its sides. Its corners were adorned with white tassels knotted in some kind of macramé pattern. Kalman rose to his feet and, in one sweeping gesture, loosely furled the tallis around and over his head. Then, after standing in silence inside the little tent for a minute or two, he let the cloth drop from his head and onto his shoulders. Along the neck band were rows of tiny silver platelets that made a soft jingling sound when they moved. The astronomer was mesmerized. "It's beautiful," she whispered. "Would it be rude of me to ask why you stand with it over your head like that?"

"No, not at all. I learned it from watching my grandfather, but it never dawned on me to ask him why. All I know is that he did it, so I do it. I do find, now, after all these years, that the ritual centers me, calms me down."

The bar mitzvah came off without a hitch. Before she was called up onto the bima, Kalman noticed that her hands were shaking. He patted her arm and whispered, "You're going to be just fine. They'll tell you everything." After it was over, Isabel returned to her seat, relieved. Even Kalman was surprised by how involved he had become in the simple ritual.

Following the service, as they waited in the buffet line for their bagels, cream cheese, smoked fish, and noodle pudding, Kalman asked Isabel where her people had come from.

"Both my parents' families are from Brazil," she said. "They started out as merchants in Spain or Portugal, but South America gave them more elbow room."

"Portuguese merchants?"

"That's right, East Indies—some kind of international trading. I don't even remember what they sold. I do remember hearing my grandmother talk about the Dutch East Indies Trading Company. Yes, I think that that's how they got to South America, and then, around the time of the American Revolution, they came to New York."

"Very interesting. Did you know that 'Portuguese merchants' was also a common euphemism for Conversos?"

"Who?"

"Marranos, Jews who fled the Inquisition and survived by pretending to be Christians."

She was silent for a minute. Then she said, "You know, it is funny you should say that. As a child, I was very close to my father's mother. She lived with us. She's the one who taught me how to bake that fig cake you liked so much. Anyway, once, when I was just a little girl, I was helping her set the table for dinner and I placed the two candlesticks at the opposite ends of the table like I had seen in a magazine. She walked into the dining room, took one look, and put them side by side in the center. 'On Friday, they always go like this, side by side,' she said. She never explained why. I wouldn't have thought twice about it if it weren't for my college roommate, who was from a suburb of Cleveland—Shaker Heights. She came home with me once for a weekend. She was Jewish. As we were setting the table, she thanked me for being so sensitive. 'About what?' I said. 'About Shabbat,' she said. I didn't know what she was talking about until she said a Hebrew prayer and lit the candles. The next time we visited my grandmother—she was in her nineties by then—I asked her about it. She replied that her mother had always done it that way. 'It's an old family tradition,' she said. 'Oh,' I said, and never gave it another thought until just now."

"Well, you know, your family's itinerary *does* follow one of the principal migration routes of Sephardic Jews. Fleeing Spain and Portugal, many wound up first in Holland. And since Jews were dispersed throughout the world but all spoke the same language, many naturally became involved in international commerce. I think it was around 1580 or '90, with the Union of Utrecht, when a bunch of Dutch provinces became Protestant, many Sephardim immigrated to Brazil and then later found their way to America."

"Are you saying . . ."

"It's not exactly astrophysics."

"That means that my Catholic great-grandmother, Abigail Delgado . . ."

"Hey, it happened to Madeleine Albright, why not you?"

Isabel thought for a moment. "Does this mean that I'm not a shikse after all?"

"I'm afraid that is a question that could only be answered by a qualified rabbinic authority."

"You wouldn't know, by any chance, where I might find one?"

He straightened his posture and centered the knot of his necktie.

Isabel smiled. "Kalman, I really want to thank you for helping me this morning."

"How often do I get to pray next to someone who is a professional seeker after the mystery of the creation of the universe and the beginning of time?"

"You *are* serious, aren't you."

"Professor, believe me, you are much more interesting than most of the neo-Kabbalists I hang around with, and besides, *you* are talking about empirically verifiable reality."

She smiled. "Kalman, when you told me last week that you had been married, I thought I detected some sadness in your voice. Were you married for long?"

"Two and a half years. It was the happiest time of my life."

"But . . . ?" she said.

"But it ended. She left me."

"I am so sorry."

"She ran off with one of her professors."

Isabel was stopped cold.

"It's really okay," said Kalman. "I have had decades to get over it."

"But you still sound sad."

"No, reconciled, maybe. I once had a shrink who told me that the betrayal had made me afraid of intimacy, of giving myself away. He said that I fear there won't be anything of me left."

"Oh, you poor, dear man."

"Please don't misunderstand, Isabel. We all have wounds, and we all learn to live with them. I don't want there to be any confusion. I really enjoy—no, cherish your company. You are . . . the most interesting woman I . . . I have ever known. You are a breath of intellectual fresh air, but I am honestly not interested in . . . in . . . any romantic entanglements."

"Well, then," she said, regaining her composure. "That makes us a perfect pair, now, doesn't it?"

Kalman was unsure about what she meant, but as a precaution, he echoed her words. "Yes, a perfect pair," he said.

A week after the bar mitzvah, Kalman invited Isabel to join him in the Times Square twofers line for half-price theater tickets. They were talking about the neon signs on the buildings surrounding them when some guy on a bicycle stopped at the curb next to where they stood. He was wearing a T-shirt. He said he ran his own advertising agency; he claimed his wife's plane had been delayed because of thunderstorms so they couldn't celebrate her birthday. And just like that, to Isabel's astonishment, Kalman purchased the man's two center-section orchestra seats for $140—because he *trusted* his face. My God, Isabel thought, how could such a rube survive in New York City?

Later, she sat in the theater counting down the minutes before the curtain rose, certain that every couple led down the aisle would have the *real* tickets for *their* seats and Kalman would be out $140. "Relax, Isabel," he said, noticing her concern. "It's going to be okay; trust me." But she couldn't trust him any more than she could trust the stranger on the bicycle. They really were wonderful seats.

During the intermission, Isabel asked, "Who was that guy on the bicycle, anyway?"

"I think he said his name was Carl Hass. Hey, you looked at his ID, too."

"No, I don't mean his name. I mean, why did this complete stranger ride up on his bicycle and sell us theater tickets?"

"Him?" said Kalman. "Oh, he was just someone doing his job."

"Selling theater tickets in Times Square?"

"No, silly, selling *us* theater tickets. Otherwise we would've never seen the play. Isn't that obvious?"

Well, no, it wasn't obvious at all. "You don't really believe that, do you?" Isabel said.

Kalman only shrugged.

As they filed outside after the performance, Isabel was momentarily swept away from him in the crowd. When she realized that she was alone, she spun around anxiously. But there he was, ten people away, his eyes trained on her. *See?* his face seemed to say. *Don't worry, I'm still here.*

The next week they went to the movies and saw *The Sweet Hereafter*, and a few days later they attended a lecture on something about the shape of the universe. That Saturday, the rabbi and the astronomer had dinner at a French place near the entrance to the Holland Tunnel and a week later at the deli on Second Avenue. Kalman bought her matzah-ball soup and an extra-lean corned-beef sandwich with coleslaw on rye. He explained that it was like taking her on a tour of his boyhood.

CASTILE

Most of the inhabitants of Valladolid awoke from their siestas only to discover that it was still oppressively hot. Don Moshe ben Shem Tov de Guadalajara walked past the watering trough in the center of the plaza and up the hill toward the synagogue and its adjoining academy, rerouting himself, as he walked, around sleeping dogs and stray geese. Climbing even a gradual hill required dedication, devotion. It had not rained for weeks, and each infrequent breeze brought a fine, stinging dust. He stopped in a patch of shade to catch his breath. Directly across the street stood the mansion of his new pupil. Over its outer wall, he could easily see the house itself. Such wealth! At least they were generous and the woman had such an intuitive understanding of the Bible's nuance. And she was indeed very handsome.

He stood there, wondering how God could make someone so wise and yet so beautiful. He looked up at the cloudless sky, then back at the mansion across the street. And, right on cue, the curtains on one of the high second-story windows parted slowly, revealing the form of a woman. Even from a distance, it was clear she held some kind of metallic device in her hands and seemed to be examining it in the sunlight. First she held it up to her eye and looked toward the sky. Then she looked down toward the plaza, and for a moment, just a moment, she seemed to look directly at him. How could she not have seen him? He was right there, directly in her line of vision. It all happened so fast—

barely long enough for him to conjecture that he *might* have been noticed, but not long enough to be certain. Whereupon the woman stepped back, let go of the curtains, and disappeared. He remained there, in that shadow of his own confusion, for a long time, hoping she might appear again. But, of course, she did not. Nevertheless, a few days later, as he made his way up that same street, he realized he was planning to stop to catch his breath again in the same place.

The most tantalizing—and confounding—evidence about the authorship of the Zohar comes from a diary written by the thirteenth-century Kabbalist Isaac of Akko. We know, from the reports of travelers who read the diary, that it was once in the Baron Gunzburg Library in St. Petersburg. But it has since disappeared! According to their accounts, Isaac arrived in Toledo in 1305 in search of a manuscript called *The Midrash of Rabbi Shimon bar Yohai*. Isaac recounts that he heard it had fallen into the possession of a man named Moshe de Leon, whom he finds in Valladolid. De Leon swears to Isaac that the manuscript is at his home in Ávila and promises to let him see it. Isaac is ecstatic. De Leon departs first, but while on his way home, in Arévalo, de Leon dies! Isaac is crushed but pushes on for Ávila, where he locates de Leon's widow. But she insists that the book never existed and that her husband wrote the whole thing himself! Isaac of Akko records her famous words in his diary:

"Why do you tell everybody that you are copying from a book when you write from out of your own head? Would it not be bet-

ter to say that it was your own creation? Then you would get the credit." But he would reply: "If I told them my secret, they would pay no heed to my words and would not give me a penny for them." Then I said to him: "But surely you could, at least, admit that you are writing Kabbalah." And he would reply, "If I write Kabbalah, no one but Kabbalists will read beyond the first pages. But, if I conceal the Kabbalah inside a story, then people will have to read the Kabbalah to find out how the story ends. . . ."

(It is somewhat odd that she would discredit her primary source of income.) Crestfallen, Isaac leaves Ávila and comes to another town. There he meets a man who is *convinced* of the Zohar's antiquity and shares his own story:

A long time after Moshe de Leon had written lengthy extracts from the Zohar for me, I hid one but told him I lost it. I asked him for another copy. He said, "Show me the pages that preceded and followed it." And, after a few days, he gave me the recopied text, which I then compared with the first. And, down to the very letter, they were identical! Can there be a more stringent test?

So suspicion lingers down to the present day. In Zoharic studies, you might say, authorship remains a moving target.

MANHATTAN

"Damn pigeons," said Slomovitz. "I hate 'em." He got up from his seat on the park bench, flailing his arms, stomping his feet. There was a flurry of feathers and leaves. Then he sat back down and took an apple from his briefcase and turned to Kalman. "You want a half?"

"Why, thank you, Milton. Yes, I would."

Slomovitz opened a very small Swiss Army penknife on his key chain and neatly halved the piece of fruit. With his handkerchief, he wiped the blade clean. "You don't get days like this in November every year, Kal. Pretty soon it'll be time to take your galoshes out of the back of the closet."

"You're such a pessimist."

"It's a living. So, how've you been?"

Several more pigeons, meanwhile, had regrouped and appeared to be organizing for a counteroffensive.

"If you hadn't called, I'd probably have spent the afternoon in the library and missed the whole thing."

"Well, I just got to thinking about the last time we had lunch," said Slomovitz.

"Relax, Milt, I'm okay. I really did receive a volume of Zohar in that little synagogue. There really was some old guy who gave it to me. And the back cover really has come unglued and given birth to another page. And Wasserhardt's watermark man,

Rivkin, has identified the date, and as we speak, the Page is at Oxford being photographed under ultraviolet light. Milton, these are facts."

"I never said it wasn't real, Kal. It's your recollection of how you got it that's worrisome."

"I admit that how I received the book seems to be fluid, a moving target. C'mon, Milty, we all revisit moments in our past and discover that our recollections were incomplete. Surely you must have said things like 'Now that I think about it, there might have been a man standing in the shadows' or 'Of course, she did not mean this, she meant that.' There is no such thing as an event frozen in the past."

"Stern, at my age, nothing is frozen, *especially* in my memory. You sound a lot like the postmodernists who claim the act of reading happens *between* the book and the reader and that because the reader changes, so does the meaning of the words." Slomovitz got up and tossed his apple core into a trash can across the path from their bench.

"Well, as we change," said Kalman, "so the past changes with us. Each reiteration of the past is an excursion into a new land. You can't go back to the same scene because there is no *same scene*."

"Just because you're convincing doesn't mean you're sane."

"Okay, how about this?" said Kalman. "A few weeks ago, I was recounting the story about how I picked up the Livorno Zohar and I realized that some things might have happened differently. I'm sure if there had been a videocamera on the ceiling, like they have in banks, the tape would be the same each time it was played. But *what* those gestures and shadows *mean* changes with each new viewing. I'll go farther: The holier the event, the more ways it can be retold. You remember that midrash about how there were six hundred thousand Jews at Mount Sinai and therefore six hundred thousand versions of what happened? Remember that famous list in William James's *Varieties of Religious Experience*—the one where he says that every mystical experience has four qualities: ineffable, noetic, transient, and passive? Well, I'd like to add a fifth quality: inexhaustible—it has an infinity of meanings."

Realizing that Milton had been listening more intently than usual, Kalman said, "So, Doc, am I okay?"

"It's just as I feared, Stern," Slomovitz said in mock psychiatric seriousness. "There's no doubt about it: You're looney tunes."

"Coming from a Litvak like you, that's a real compliment."

A young woman walked past their park bench led by five small dogs on their leashes.

"Too bad she doesn't have a skateboard," said Kalman.

They both nodded. "You know, Kalman, in a purely rational way, of course, as you were speaking, I was reminded of a Yom Kippur I spent at my sister's place out in L.A.—you know, Sheila, the weaver. The weather out there is always beautiful. If it weren't for the earthquakes and smog . . ."

"What about her husband? You can't stand him."

"Okay, earthquakes, smog, *and Harvey*. So, their synagogue was putting on a building addition, but the project ran over and it wasn't going to be finished in time for the High Holy Days. Their only option was to rent the local municipal auditorium, but because there was a previously scheduled performance of *Camelot*, they had to be out by six p.m."

"*Great Moments in American Judaism*, chapter twenty-nine . . ."

"The rabbi even joked during the announcements:'We must conclude our worship by six p.m. this evening, otherwise our closing hymn will be'What Do the Simple Folk Do?' But since it also meant that they could break their fasts an hour early, there were no complaints. As I walked out, I looked back at the stage. They had a choral riser, an ark for the Torah scrolls, flowers, a special backdrop. The room had been transformed into a prayer hall. But now, stagehands were carting everything away. Within minutes, the holy scenery was gone. The backdrop was raised, revealing a curtain with a castle on it. Where the ark had been, there was a drawbridge. Men were setting up suits of armor and pennants. Then I realized that the other stage set had been there *all along*, waiting. It dawned on me," said Milton,"that people can only handle one thing at a time. And that's what's so dangerous about mysticism."

Kalman tried not to agree with too much enthusiasm. "Did you ever see *Places in the Heart?*"

"Where Sally Field is trying to hang on to her farm after her husband gets murdered and John Malkovich is a blind guy who helps her?"

"Remember the closing scene where the whole cast is singing a hymn in this little southern church? The camera slowly pans the room for one last look at the characters. But there is Sally Field's husband who got killed at the beginning of the movie, sitting right there with the kid who accidentally killed him, and no one seems to notice. The singing *and* the weeping are simultaneous."

"Stern, you should've been a film critic."

"Milt, it happens all at once. But we can't handle everything all at once, so we filter it down to one thing at a time. Think about it. . . . You see someone born . . . a great joy. You see someone die: That's very sad. But if . . . we had the death *and* the birth at the same time, intolerable . . . it would be terrible. Our circuitry would get fried."

While Kalman took a few deep breaths, Milt got a faraway look in his eyes. "No argument there, Kal. Birth *and* death are *within* each other. Joy contains sadness; sadness, joy."

"From God's perspective, everything happens all at once. That's why it's so frightening to see God, because then you get it all at once, too. For God, history is a stack of transparencies. God looks straight down through the whole pile. From that perspective, you can't cry because you know you will laugh. You can't laugh because you know the price that will be paid. Like you said, Milt, there are an infinite inventory of stage settings. And religion is a way of trying to understand how the present backdrop is precisely what has been specified by the playwright. You say, 'Oh, *now* I understand. Everything is the way it's supposed to be.' You may not like it, but you understand."

After a few moments, Kalman said, "The wedding invitation is glued over an obituary, and beneath the obituary is a birth announcement—one transparent layer over another. The only question is: How many can you handle at once?"

"That is the difference between a Litvak like me and a mystic like you. I want everything, but I want it one thing at a time. You want Nothing with a capital N, but you want it all at once. That reminds me, I've got to go have an argument with the registrar."

"Why don't you try yelling in Yiddish; that ought to slow her down."

"Very funny, Stern, very funny. Hey, how is your new girl-friend, the astronomer lady?"

"I told you, Milton, she is *not* my girlfriend. Maybe I'll get her to join us for lunch sometime."

Both men rose and collected their things.

"Oh, I almost forgot," said Slomovitz. "Any word yet from Oxford?"

"Still nothing."

"It's been months."

"Rivkin told Wasserhardt something about his guy being on vacation and then a big backlog."

"Well, let me know when Captain Ultraviolet resurfaces."

"I promise. And Milt, watch out for the pigeons; they can get very aggressive towards the end of autumn."

Kalman set off down Fourth Street. But he did not return directly to his office. Instead he found another bench, closed his eyes, and went to Israel.

SAFED: FOURTH ITERATION

An old man, wearing a robe striped with very narrow maroon and yellow vertical lines signifying to the cognoscenti that he had been born in Jerusalem, appeared in the doorway of the small synagogue. He acknowledged Kalman with a cautious nod and began sweeping the floor. The slow shuffle of his slippers sounded like fine-grain sandpaper on the stone floor. Under his breath he kept mumbling a little ditty. Kalman, meanwhile, pretended he was just another tourist admiring the architecture and fiddling with the controls on his camera. He was transfixed by the janitor. The broom work seemed to be collecting nothing. And then Kalman understood why: The floor was spotless; it did not need sweeping! As he moved closer, Kalman was able to discern the lyrics to the nursery rhyme:

There once was a man
Who discovered a book,
It had so many layers
He didn't know where to look.

"That's English you're singing," Kalman said.

"And English you're speaking."

"Why are you singing in English?"

"Because you don't understand Aramaic."

"How do you know that?"

"You'd be surprised."

"Try me."

"In a moment, you're going to ask me if I have any old books on mysticism."

"I'm looking for some old books on Kabbalah. . . ."

The old man nodded with a smile and walked over to a table cluttered with books and rubbish. "Here's a nice one—thirteenth-century Provence." He blew off the dust. "A good book always conceals more than it reveals. People have to work their way up to its awareness. If you tell them right away, if you make it too easy, they will not believe it. You must whisper it to them like it's some kind of big secret. For instance, if I were to tell you that the *Ayn Sof*—Infinite Nothing—began creation with a spark of impenetrable darkness, a *botzina d'qardinuta*, and the womb of a world that is coming, *alma d'ah-tay*, you'd say, 'Ho hum.' But if I showed it to you here inside a book"— he reached into the pile, picked up another old volume, and opened it—"a book like this, that seems to be very old and has mysteriously come into your hand, then you would pay it careful attention, would you not?"

Kalman craned his neck to see if he could confirm the text. It did indeed contain the phrases *botzina d'qardinuta* and *alma d'ah-tay*.

"May I hold it?"

"Why not?" replied the old man. "It's yours; has your name on it." He handed Kalman the book and went back to sweeping the floor:

> *There once was a man*
> *Who discovered a book,*
> *It had so many layers*
> *He didn't know where to look.*

"This is not happening," said Kalman. "This is not real. I need some external proof here, some kind of sign. . . ."

"I already gave you a book. Now you want a sign, too?"

"Well, yes. I *would* like a sign."

"I'm sorry, but you've got it all wrong. No one is given a sign—not Moses at the bush, not the Israelites at the Red Sea. The natural order does not change, ever. The only things that do change are your own eyes: You see in a new way."

Kalman thought, Maybe the caretaker is himself a sign.

"Everything's a sign," the old man replied, as if Kalman had spoken out loud. "Actually, it might be more accurate to say that you yourself become a sign painter. You suddenly see what has been there all along. You don't understand it so much as you enter it. You walk *inside* the sign. You permit it to envelop you. You permit it to transform you. Then you look back on it, sometimes months, years, even decades later, and you realize that you were 'taken in.' That's when you became someone new."

"You are saying," said Kalman, "that then I see what has been there all along."

"You want a sign?" said the old man. "Look out the window."

Kalman looked out the window.

"Tell me what you see."

"I see the courtyard, a stairway, a tree. . . ."

"Pick one."

"Which one?"

"Any one. It doesn't really matter."

"What do you mean, it doesn't really matter?"

"Trust me. Just pick a card, any card."

Kalman picked the stairway.

"Okay, it's a sign."

"No, it's not. It's just a stairway."

The old man gestured in the other direction into the prayer hall. "Then look over there."

Kalman followed his instructions.

"What do you pick this time?"

Kalman picked the paneless windows.

"So go ahead. Enter the sign."

"You want me to walk out the window?"

"No, no. Just permit yourself to let the windows be a window to another way of seeing the world."

"You're telling me that everything is a sign?"

"No, not exactly. In theory, of course, anything *could* be a sign. But in reality, what's a sign for one person usually turns out to be just an object for someone else."

"Well, that means that anything can be anything."

"That's mysticism for you."

"It's also silly."

"You want serious? Call your accountant."

Kalman looked at the book in his hands, the one with his name on it.

The old man went back to his sweeping.

There once was a man
Who discovered a book,
It had so many layers
He didn't know where to look.

MANHATTAN

In 1910, Georges Claude, a French chemist and inventor, demonstrated to the Paris public that by applying an electrical charge to a sealed tube of neon gas, he could create a lamp. As a lamp, it wasn't much to write home about, but as a medium of outdoor advertising, it initiated a revolution. Claude's new glass tubes lit the main entrance to the Paris Opéra in red and blue. The color scheme became known as *les couleurs Opéra* and would exert a powerful aesthetic influence on the first two decades of the nascent art deco movement. Thirteen years later, the Claude Neon Company sold its first two gas signs in the United States to Earle C. Anthony, who owned an automobile dealership in Los Angeles. The signs said: PACKARD. Unlike prior forms of electrically lit advertising, neon signs were visible in daylight! Neon gas glows with a characteristic red light, but with the addition of elements such as argon, mercury, and phosphor, chemists can produce every color of the rainbow. But it is red, still produced by neon, that remains the brightest way to write in light. In the early days, people called the new signs "liquid fire."

Now, of course, the signs are everywhere. The Tower Records sign Kalman can see from his Zohar seminar room up on the fifth floor, for example, is red neon. So is the center of the big Citgo sign over Kenmore Square in Boston near where Kalman grew up.

Through the music in his headphones, Kalman had momentarily lost track again of where he ended and the rest of the universe began. Music was everywhere, and he was it. By the time he returned from wherever it was he had been, there were tears in his eyes. He glanced at his watch to see how long he'd been gone (ten minutes, the last seven of which he did not remember at all). He set the earphones back on the rack and looked around surreptitiously at the half dozen other shoppers in the classical music department to see if anyone had noticed. Satisfied his secret was still safe, he picked up a CD of Robert Schumann's *Three Romances for Oboe and Piano, Op. 94.*

"Thanks for telling me about this one," he said to the Latino clerk wearing a Hawaiian shirt who stood behind the cash register.

"Yo, my oboe man—any time."

Kalman watched the clerk staple the cash register receipt across the top of the bright yellow-and-red plastic bag. He walked downstairs to the main floor, claimed his valise from the attendant at the counter, and walked outside onto Broadway, still humming the Schumann. The sun was shining. He turned around and looked up at the big red neon Tower Records sign. Then he looked at the gargoyles on the building across the street. He looked at a man selling fruit from a pushcart. He listened to the siren of a fire engine going up Lafayette. He watched a bicycle messenger with what must have been a twenty-pound lock and chain slung over his shoulder dart in and out of traffic. He glanced up at the blinking orange DON'T WALK sign on the other side of Broadway. "Well," he sighed, "at least if I'm not going to get a sign before I die, I will always have the Page." And even though it was still with Rivkin's friend somewhere in England, the Page indeed was his. It was tangible proof that Kalman Stern was a bona fide recipient of ancient truth. Indeed, if you had asked him to identify his most precious possession, he would have been able to answer without a moment's hesitation.

Isabel's search for a sign was much less desultory, but equally intense. She knew that, contrary to all reason, she needed some external corroboration for what she felt. One, after all, does not embark on a major new adventure in life without carefully assembling all the relevant data and assessing all the risks.

She continued driving slowly down the gravel road and into a small parking area. She shut off the ignition. But she did not get out. Instead, she looked out at the last dry leaves of November. With most of the foliage off the trees now, the sun was brighter, but its light was cold. "This is silly," she said to herself, put her scarf around her neck, and opened the car door. It was colder than she had anticipated. She buttoned the neck of her coat and snugged a knit hat down over her ears. In the distance, she heard a train go by on an elevated subway line. She reached into her coat pocket and found the photocopied map. It took her a few moments to orient herself to its symbols. "A map of the known universe," she said to the leaves blowing by. She walked past monuments of all shapes and sizes, some festooned with bouquets of flowers and American flags, others untended, overgrown, covered with leaves. But every stone had a name. "A convention of known planets, each with its own name and celestial coordinates in eternity," she mused.

A few more rows, one jog to the left, and she stopped and read the inscription on the monument before her: "Marta Benveniste, Beloved Wife and Mother, 1929–1965." Etched below that was a three-word question that Isabel herself had chosen as a child, decades before: "Who created these?" She stooped and brushed away some leaves from the modest stone. Then, looking this way and that to make sure she was alone, she spoke to it: "I am sorry I have not come here for so long. Oh,

Mother, can you hear me? When you decided to marry Daddy, how did you know? Oh, how I wish you could tell me. . . ."

She listened to the barely audible sound of the wind in the trees. She was grateful for the silence. Something tiny and light brushed her cheek. And, as if looking for a warm place to spend the night, it lodged itself between her scarf and the skin of her neck with a tiny crackle. But it was only a leaf. Isabel removed it carefully, examined it for a moment, and then released it to the breeze. And, quickly lost amid all the others, it was gone.

That evening after dinner, Kalman suggested they walk instead of taking a cab. Their conversation turned to nature when a sparrow, startled off its nighttime perch, practically landed on Kalman's head.

"Birds," Isabel said. "I will tell you about birds. I have an old friend who's an ornithologist, a really big-time birder. A few winters ago, she persuaded me to join her on a bird-watching trip."

"Like golf, it's just an excuse to walk in nature."

"I used to think that, too. At the time I was sick of the city and needed a change of scenery; she's a good companion, so I went. We flew out to Albuquerque, rented a car, and drove to a little bed-and-breakfast near the entrance to a place called the Bosque del Apache, Forest of the Apache, a bird sanctuary in the middle of the desert. Next morning, we got up at four forty-five a.m.—I still don't believe I did this—and drove into the park, where there were already dozens of cars. Kal, there must have been fifty cameras set up on tripods. We stood out there shivering in the darkness, sipping coffee from a thermos. Off in the distance, you could just make out the horizon, a thin dark ribbon of red. And then, in only a few seconds, the whole sky exploded into bright orange. I had never in my life seen such brilliant color in the sky."

"Must've been awesome," said Kalman.

"It was. But it was also nothing compared with what came next. Within the next ten minutes, we all watched in awestruck silence as twenty-five thousand snow geese, cranes, and great blue herons awoke from sleeping on the water and flew off for the next leg of their migration! Kalman . . ." She stopped walking and faced him directly. "They were so close and there were so many of them, I could literally feel the wing-flung wind on my face!"

"Oh, my God!"

Isabel's smile was beatific. Kalman reached out and, as if he were hoping to share the experience, caressed her cheek.

"I know. It's incredible," said Isabel. "Even when I describe it myself, I don't believe it. The night before, the park rangers had warned us: 'You are never the same after the "flyaway." ' But I didn't believe them until I saw for myself. And then I understood. And here's the part that humbles me, Kalman. The birds, they do it all the time. Whether we're there to watch them or not; they land in the waters of the Bosque, and come first light they fly away. And they do it year after year after year." As she spoke, her eyes grew moist. "They do it just like the great whales move through the waters of the sea and mitochondria swim through the fluid within our cells. Everywhere there are these great flowing streams of life, currents of creatures, all doing what they were *meant* to do, one great orchestrated flow of life. My God, Kalman, the only words I could find were, 'Who created these?' "

"That's what you told me your mother said, isn't it."

"And it's what you said was in the Zohar, right?"

"Yes. '*Mi vara ayleh?*' 'Who created these?'"

"I remember you said the Book of Isaiah."

"Go to the head of the class. But your story reminds me of another Zohar passage. You know that the holiest day of the year in Judaism is Yom Kippur."

Isabel nodded.

"Well, that was also the only time when the high priest was permitted to enter the holy of holies, the innermost chamber of the temple in Jerusalem. And he only had to do one thing—pronounce the ineffable Name of God—'the One who brings into being all that is.' And the room in which he would utter this name was so sacred that if, God forbid, the poor man should drop dead of a heart attack while he was inside, no one could go back in to retrieve his corpse! The Zohar explains that they solved the problem by tying a rope around his leg! Then the legend goes on to say that once the high priest entered the holy of holies, even *he* closed his eyes—so as not to gaze where it was forbidden. But as cherubim sang their praises, he was able to hear the sound of the flapping of their wings."

"Rabbi, are you saying I was in the holy of holies?"

THE TEXT OF *THE BOOK OF LOVE*

"Alex, I keep forgetting to tell you," said Kalman when they met in the library. "I started reading that *Book of Love* article you gave me. It's very good. They sure don't write mysticism like *that* anymore. Where'd you find it?"

"It showed up in a box of papers and pamphlets that Dr. Harkavy donated to us when he retired. I especially liked the part about losing yourself. While I was cataloging, it caught my eye. And when I read it, I said to myself, 'Kalman should read this.' Right away, it made me think about you."

"About me?"

Alex rolled a mug of tea back and forth in his palms. "Kalman, I could ask you a question, *nicht?*"

"Since when did you ever ask my permission?"

"How long has it been?"

"Been since what?"

"You know what I mean, since Elaine."

Kalman pursed his lips in resigned annoyance. "Nineteen years, Alex. Nineteen years this April, why?"

"Because it has been such a long time. First you were afraid, I understand this, but now, now you have even maybe forgotten *how* to give of yourself again. You have been living alone for so many years. And Kalman, if you don't get loving, then there is no new life and maybe there is no God, either."

"Loving and God?"

"*Jah!* That is why I gave you the article. For both to love and to find God, you must annihilate your self. If you still hold on to your self, then it isn't love. And I think, if you still hold on to your self, then you don't find God, either."

"Whatever happened to two autonomous, individuated selves coming together?"

"Sure, it always starts with two separate people. But if it ends there, it's only, how do you say it, an intimate business partner-ship." Wasserhardt closed his eyes for a moment. "Kalman, al-most ten years ago I lost my Rochele. There isn't a day when I don't think about her. But me, I'm an old man. You, on the other hand, are not. Kalman, for there to be real loving, the giver must become the gift. *Fahrstaesen sie?*"

Kalman nodded, but not because he understood.

That evening, waiting for the subway, Kalman began reading the actual text of *The Book of Love*:

> THEREFORE THE MAIDENS LOVE YOU . . . (*Songs* 1:3). *Therefore do worlds love you—one generation after another, a love transcending lifetimes. Every soul is connected to every other, not merely during one's own lifetime, but also through all generations.*
>
> *The experiences of other souls appear in our own lives just as ours will show up in generations yet to come. In this way, a soul's experience of long ago might also, for a few minutes, dwell within someone living now. Suddenly he knows or seems to re-member something that he could not possibly have experienced. These memories survive the forgetting that seems to separate one lifetime from another. And yet, in the soul of the one for whom it is intended, the memory can blossom and bring forth fruit in a new season.*

Without lifting his head, Kalman surreptitiously raised his eyes to see if anyone was watching him. As if, at the Astor

Place uptown station at five-thirty on a weekday afternoon, amid, conservatively, a few hundred other passengers, anyone would even notice him at all. Anxious the train might come before he could finish the section, Kalman quickly read the last paragraph.

> In the words of the holy Zohar III:71a–b: *Even though a righteous person departs from this world, he is not removed from or deprived of all the worlds, because he continues to exist in all the worlds even more than during his own life-time. . . . As it is written in Song of Songs 1:3,* THE MAIDENS LOVE YOU. *Do not read* alamot—*maidens*—*but* olamot—*worlds.* THE WORLDS LOVE YOU. *Happy is their portion.*

"Not only do we inherit and bequeath memories," said Kalman, "this means that we can also complete undone deeds of previous generations. And the holy part is that, since it's all anonymous, no one will ever know."

And that is what he wrote in the margin: "To complete un-done deeds of previous generations."

"And no one will ever know," he said as if he were addressing the fragment.

MANHATTAN

"I am sorry, Isabel," Kalman said over dinner the next week, "but rejecting a God up in heaven who is supposed to run the world does not make you an atheist. It only means you have renounced classical theism."

"Then what *do* you mean when *you* talk about God?"

"There are two ways to understand our relationship with God. The first is classical theism—the one you reject. In that model, God can be represented as a big circle." Kalman drew one on her place mat. "And you a little circle below it." He drew a tiny circle under the big one. "In this model God is *other* than creation, *above* it, and runs it. He—and since it's so hierarchical, God is a 'He'—may be actively involved or criminally absent. He can be doing a good job or a lousy one. Such a God can tell us to do things—don't murder, give charity, be nice—and we can tell God things, too—let me pass the exam, please make Johnny well again, stop war. In such a system, good people are supposed to get rewarded and bad people punished. But the key thing here is that God is *other* than the created world—above and beyond it."

She nodded. It was her scientist face.

"It turns out, however," Kalman said, "that there is another model. It has a more Eastern ring, but it has been around in Western religion, too. In this model, God is still a big circle." He drew another big circle on the place mat, but this time he drew the little circle *inside* the bigger one. "The little circle, here, still represents you, but see, it is *within* the big circle of God. You would call this mystical monism. It's all one and it's all God. God is simply all there is. And therefore, the separateness of anyone or anything is *illusory* because *everything* is a manifestation of God! God is the ocean, and we are the waves."

"But how can you pray to something of which you are already a manifestation?"

"Well, if prayer is a conversation between two discrete parties, then you can't. But prayer can also be an opportunity to contemplate your presence *within* the divine All. God is the One through whom everyone and everything is joined to every one and every thing. What did the mystic say to the hot-dog vendor?"

Isabel shrugged.

"Make me *one* with everything."

He watched her expression change from bafflement to delight.

"Do you see? When you are in a place like that," said Kalman, "then everything is simply the way it is."

"But then what does it mean to say that you believe in God?" said Isabel. "It certainly cannot mean that you are asserting the existence of some nonempirically verifiable entity."

"Excellent. If you're a mystic, saying you believe in God means that you have an abiding suspicion that everything is a manifestation of God, and no matter how horrific it might be, it is still, somehow, filled with holiness. You may not be able to see it, but the meaning is there; the filaments of eternity are not only interwoven and interdependent, but they all have a singular source."

But now, instead of shining with the brightness of comprehension, Isabel's eyes reddened. She coughed, excused herself, and went to the ladies' room. Kalman froze. Uh-oh, I have said something wrong, he thought. But what? People do not get this upset over theology. . . .

When she returned, Kalman rose and helped her with her chair. "It was something I said, wasn't it."

"There's no way you could have known." Isabel blew her nose, took a drink of water. "They never even told me how it happened."

Kalman listened intently.

"I suppose I can't really blame them. I was only eight. Everyone just said that my thirty-six-year-old mother died of a heart attack."

"Yes, I remember. You told me she was a very spiritual woman."

"Well, even as a little girl, the story didn't quite hang together. But I didn't have the words to say I didn't buy it. So I never told anyone. It wasn't until I was in high school that I finally went down to the public library and looked up the newspaper account for myself. That was when I found out how my mother *really* died. Kalman, it wasn't a heart attack. My spiritual, religious mother was struck and killed by a taxi on Twenty-fifth Street! It was so random, so meaningless. The article said that the cabbie was drunk and that his fare was a young man on vacation, a high school science teacher from Dorchester, Massachusetts, who actually attended her funeral."

"I am so sorry, Isabel."

"I'm okay now," she said. "But that afternoon it was like my mother died all over again."

"You want to know something crazy?" said Kalman. "*I* went to high school in Dorchester, Massachusetts, in 1965. I had this terrific science teacher named Arnold Smolens. Did the article identify the man in the taxicab?"

Isabel shook her head. "No, only that he was a science teacher from Dorchester. The only people it named were my mother and my father and me."

Kalman crumpled his paper napkin. "C'mon," he said, "let's get out of here."

"No, it's all right. We can stay. I felt I needed to tell you, that's all."

"Your skepticism about religion certainly now makes a lot more sense."

She finished her water. The waiter filled her glass again.

"Kal, besides her, I've never known someone who trusts the universe the way you do. When I am with you, I feel like the universe has whispered, 'Everything is going to be okay.' It makes me feel less fearful, less timid."

Kalman smiled. "Isabel, what I'm about to say will not explain her death or apologize for God, but it does bring me some solace, and maybe it will for you, too."

She nodded.

"It's an old Hasidic story," he said. "There was once a man who went to his rebbe, his spiritual master, because his life was filled with suffering. After describing in detail his many woes, the rabbi sighed in sympathy. 'Oh, my friend, I cannot possibly help someone who has so much grief. You should seek out the advice of Reb Zusya. His life also has been strewn with tragedy.' The man thanked his rebbe and set out in search of this new teacher. But when he recounted his misfortunes, Zusya only looked at him in puzzlement. 'Why have you come to me?' he said. 'I don't understand; I have never experienced suffering.' "

Kalman smiled. "I hope that wasn't too theological. . . ."

"No. As a matter of fact, I think it is a very wise story. People get what they get; it's not about what they deserve, but about how they receive it."

Kalman did not speak. Instead, he reached across the table and took her hands in his.

"Kalman," she said, "how do Jews learn this?"

"They read and interpret and argue over the meaning of sacred texts."

"But you don't seem to take scripture literally. . . ."

"The Zohar—remember, fourteenth century, Castile—is already way ahead of us. Six centuries ago, its author says that the stories in the Torah couldn't be about what they seem to be about, because otherwise we could write better stories!"

Isabel laughed out loud. "It really says that?"

"Verbatim."

"But then how do you know how to read Scripture?"

"Wait," he said, fumbling in his jacket pockets. "I have the answer in my pocket!" He produced a photocopied page. "It's a Zohar translation I've been preparing for a lecture." He handed it to her.

There is a beautiful woman, hidden in her palace. She has a lover. No one else knows; the whole thing is clandestine. And because of his great longing for her, he continually passes the entrance to her mansion looking and waiting. She knows he is walking back and forth by the entrance. What does she do? She opens the door of that hidden palace just a little bit and shows her face to him. Then she quickly closes it and hides again. No one else sees or even notices what's going on, only the one who loves

*her. And his heart and soul, his inner being, flows after her. He
knows that because of his love for her, she has revealed herself to
him for this one moment to awaken him. . . . In this way Torah
reveals and conceals herself; she does what she does to awaken
love in her lover. Finally, once he has become accustomed to her,
she reveals herself to him, face-to-face. She speaks of all her hidden mysteries, all the hidden ways, long ago concealed within her
heart. . . . Now he understands why he must not add to those
words or take any away. . . .*

"It's so wise, so romantic!" she said. "Courtly love as a
metaphor for religious reading."

"It's more than just romance. Kabbalah brought sex back
into Jewish theology. Up until then, the God of the Jews was
a disembodied deity who hadn't had anything erotic happen
to Him since before the creation of the world. After the
Zohar, God was androgynous! Now, the yearning of two
lovers to make new life is present *within* God, too. The Holy
Oneness of All Being continuously experiences eros *within* itself. And not only that, but this coupling, this fusion of male
and female, can be encouraged by sacred deeds of which human sexuality is—alas, only rarely—an example."

And that was when Dr. Isabel Benveniste, senior research
astronomer at Columbia University, decided that she was
done with being cautious.

FIVE

LIVORNO

There were already many Kabbalists in the town of Leghorn by the middle of the seventeenth century, but Raphael Mendoza was not one of them. He had no time for such nonsense. He barely had time for his weekly regimen of Torah and Mishnah. Raphael was a businessman chronically struggling to turn a profit, who, as fate would have it, wound up running a Hebrew publishing house on Agrippa Street. His wife said, "Raphael, why do you waste your energy on trying to make books for Jews?" He would reply, "Because your father, his memory is a blessing, wasted *his* energy trying to make books for Jews, and when I married you, his business was part of *your* dowry. And besides, I love making Jewish books almost as much as I love making love to you." Then she would be silent.

Leghorn is the main port of the north-central Italian state of Tuscany on the Ligurian Sea. At the beginning of the sixteenth century, it was just another malaria-ridden village. Then the Medici decided to try to attract foreigners who might help them make it over into a commercial center. After several false starts and many improvements to the town and its port, the Medici decided to sweeten the deal. They guaranteed Jewish immigrants Tuscan citizenship, freedom for Marranos to return to Judaism, and an exemption from wearing the Jewish badge. It worked. Jewish immigration grew steadily until Jews constituted the largest and most influential segment of the city's mercantile class. Because most were Marranos tracing their ancestry back through North Africa or Turkey to Iberia, Portuguese and Spanish became the de facto languages. Leghorn also became a major center for making books. Its principal industries included paper manufacture and Hebrew printing. The first Hebrew press was established there in the middle of the seventeenth century, and within the next hundred years, the imprimaturs of sixteen additional Jewish publishing houses appeared on the title pages of books throughout the Mediterranean. To this day, even though all of its presses have long since relocated to Israel, because many of the original plates are still used, the Leghorn—or, as it is called in Italian, Livorno—imprint continues to appear in newly published volumes.

Raphael Mendoza had let his apprentice go home early, and all he had to do was what he had mistakenly assumed would be an easy job. The next morning, Signor David Cassuto, easily Raphael's best customer, would arrive to collect the Zohar he had been promised and which he had paid for in advance. All the signatures had already been assembled, sewn, and trimmed. Raphael began heating the glue and wiped down the press for the final binding. On the shelf, right where they were supposed to be, were the leather covers already embossed for Exodus and Leviticus-Numbers-Deuteronomy and . . . Where was the cover for volume one, Genesis? Finally he found most of it on the other bench. But the boy had apparently run out of board stock for the back cover and left it unfinished. "I need one more cover," Raphael said to no one. "You are a publisher. You can solve this problem. You have the glue; you can manufacture the board stock from scratch." He took a deep breath, wiped his forehead, and picked up several sheets of heavy scrap paper, squeezing them tightly together between his thumb and forefinger. "Still thinner than the front cover."

Rummaging through the papers on the workbench, Mendoza found two inventory sheets, a letter from his brother-in-law in Benghazi, a bill to the thief de Modena that probably would *never* be paid, and one other sheet of notes—a page of Kabbalistic nonsense, maybe some kind of letter. "More Kabbalah," he mumbled with contempt. "It's everywhere in this city." Then, addressing the page, Mendoza said, "You will give your life so that Signor Cassuto can have his Zohar tomorrow morning and I can feed my children." He slid it in amid the stack of other papers he had collected. The contents of the glue pot were still warm. His father-in-law had long ago whispered to him that a bit of sugar added to the paste would further increase its adhesive properties. He daubed each sheet with the adhesive, folded and trimmed the leather, arranged sheets of decorative colored pastedowns on the top and bottom, placed the whole pile squarely into the box frame, closed its lid, and rotated the wheel of the press that would transform the gooey bundle into one single piece of cardboard for the back cover of volume one of the Zohar.

The next morning, Raphael Mendoza removed the finished volume from the box press and admired his work. If he did say so himself, it was a beautiful book. Then, just as a precaution, to make sure no glue had accidentally seeped in between any of the pages, he fanned them, first one way and then the other. During the second pass, he caught two fused leaves. Using his finger, he separated them carefully. That was when his eye caught one phrase that, for a moment, seemed to him to be not in Aramaic, but—how odd—in Italian. It said: "*Capolavoro. Ben fatto!*"—"A masterpiece. Well done!" But then, after he rubbed his eyes and looked again closely, there was only Aramaic. "Kabbalah," he said, "phooey!"

MANHATTAN

"Kalman, the reason you're lonely," Slomovitz had said, "is not because you refuse to let anyone in, but because you're afraid to give *yourself* away. Maybe you really just like being in control." And, like most people confronting discomfiting truths about themselves, Kalman had laughed it off. But now, several days later, he could still hear Milt's trenchant observation. And each time he did, the words were more painful than the last time.

"How much for the roses? The yellow ones over there," Kalman said, pointing to a bunch on the top shelf of the makeshift cart.

The street-corner florist looked away. "It's already the end of the day. Ten bucks, they're all yours."

"You got anything nicer?"

"Maybe these pink ones here?"

They were a little healthier. "No," said Kalman, "I think I'll stick with the yellow." He counted out two fives. The man wrapped them in green tissue and then stapled the bunch.

"You want a ribbon?"

"No thanks."

He started to walk away but turned back.

"Yeah. I changed my mind. I'll take the ribbon. Maybe you could make a bow?"

Kalman walked through the main gate of Columbia University at 116th Street. He turned left up the steps in front of the old library (the one the students occupied back in the 1960s) and walked north to Pupin Hall. If there were any security guards, they were taking a very long coffee break. He took the elevator to the fourteenth floor. At least he was alone. But instead of walking down the hall and surprising Isabel in her office, he noticed a small sign on the stairwell door that said, OBSERVATORY, ONE FLIGHT UP.

"Just one flight," he said to himself, and walked up the stairway to the roof. He opened the big metal door and stepped out into the crisp November night. In front of him was an astronomical observatory. He walked over to the western edge of the roof where there was a waist-high brick wall. Kalman could see the spires of Riverside Church, Grant's Tomb, the Hudson River, and the lights along the top of Palisades over in Jersey. Even with the lights of the city, hundreds of stars were visible. Turning around, he thought he might find a similar view from the other direction, but instead he found himself face-to-face with a security guard.

"What are you doing up here?"

Kalman's mouth went dry. "Just admiring . . . the view."

"Well, I'm sorry, mister, but people aren't allowed up here unless they have a pass. You'll have to—"

The door clicked open and both men turned around. A woman, silhouetted by the bright light of the stairwell with a coat over her shoulders, stepped through the metal doorway and onto the roof.

"Kalman! I thought that was you in the corridor. What are you doing up here?"

"Just admiring the view," Kalman said, embarrassed.

Surrounded by light, she looked beatific, radiant.

"It's an incredible view."

The guard frowned. "You know this guy, Professor?"

"Yes, I do. It's okay, Jorge. He's a friend of mine."

"He's gotta have a pass, you know."

"I know. I'll take care of it, Jorge."

"Whatever you say, Professor." The guard took an officious

look around the rest of roof and disappeared through the doorway.

Behind her, framing her head like a halo, Kalman saw the metallic dome of the observatory. At the same time, Isabel noticed the flowers in his hand.

"Here," he said, holding out the roses. "On the street . . . some guy . . ."

"Oh, Kalman, yellow, my favorite. They're beautiful."

But Kalman only looked over her shoulder, relieved to have something else to talk about. "Observatory . . . Is that the telescope?" he asked.

Isabel turned to see what he was looking at. "Students use it."

"Not professors?"

"I use an electronic feed from Puerto Rico and a digital computer display. But optical scopes are still important for beginning astronomers; they give you a sense of history. Even a little scope like this one, amid all the lights of the city, can provide a powerful experience."

"Really?"

"Oh, yes. Would you like to have a look?"

"You could . . . do that? I mean . . ."

"Sure I could. The last class left hours ago. Let's see . . . Philbrick was using it for a project, but he's visiting his mother in Des Moines. We have it all to ourselves."

He followed her across Pupin's roof. From a jailer's ring of keys in her purse, she found one that fit. He held open the door for her, then let it close with a clank behind them. Isabel turned on the lights and climbed a short, steep metal staircase, Kalman right behind her. It was a little warmer, but not much.

"Ready?" she said.

"Yes, ma'am."

She switched off the white lights and turned on the reds. But even in the dim crimson glow, Kalman could see that she had reached around behind her waist and was unfastening the snap on her skirt.

It wasn't until afterward, as they lay on the floor next to the space heater, her head on his shoulder, that they realized how cold the concrete actually was. He reached over, folding his jacket up into a pillow, and looked up at the telescope. The red lights reflected on the shiny metal looked vaguely ominous.

On their way out of the dome, Isabel stooped and picked up the roses. A few had already begun to lose their petals. They left a dotted yellow trail on the black tar roof, connecting the observatory dome with the stairwell door.

In the taxi on the way back to her apartment, they barely spoke. Kalman held her hand with chivalrous determination; Isabel smiled with polite formality.

CASTILE: FIFTH ITERATION

"Don Manuel, tell me, please, where did you find this scrap of parchment?" said Moshe ben Shem Tov de Guadalajara to the custodian of the small Castilian synagogue-academy.

"Which one?"

"This one here with these phrases—*botzina d'qardinuta* and *alma d'ah-tay*—written on it?"

Don Manuel squinted. "The people of Israel," he said with a dismissive shrug, "they never throw away anything with writing on it. It might contain God's Name. And besides, even if the parchment doesn't have God's Name, you could always erase what's been written and write something else. It's a new piece of parchment. May I see for myself?"

Moshe handed him the brittle sheet of animal skin. The old man examined it—first with the tips of his fingers, caressing its texture, and then with his eyes, trying to decipher its barely legible letters.

"Oh, *this* one," he said. "I think it must be very old. See, you can tell from the color and the thickness. I wouldn't be at all surprised if it were Talmudic, maybe even Mishnaic."

The young Kabbalist counted the ages in his head. "You saying Shimon bar Yohai?"

"It could be from the third century, maybe even earlier."

"Are you telling me that there are pieces of writing that were created before the authors of the Talmud just lying over there on the table in the corner? Are there any more?"

"The fragments on the table, they are all from the *geniza*. Sometimes, you know how it is, I check to make sure that what is there was not left by mistake. The custodian before me, I worry he might have been a little sloppy. But it is too dark down there for these old eyes to read, so I bring a pile upstairs, and when I find a free moment, I examine the scraps in the light. Do you want me to look again?"

"You would do that? Oh, yes. Please."

Whereupon the custodian lit a lantern and carefully lifted open a wooden trapdoor. Moshe watched him descend a ladder into the darkness within which all books are initially hidden. And then, from the darkness: "Would you perhaps like to see for yourself?"

Moshe got down on his hands and knees and peered down into the cellar. He could just make out several stacks of lumber and, carved into the stone walls, some shelves stuffed with what looked like parchment and parts of scrolls, your ordinary *geniza* rubbish. The caretaker placed the lantern on a crate, stooped down, and began rummaging through one of the lower shelves. Moshe thought of the prayer hall above them, with all its ornate wood carvings and finely woven tapestries. That whole building stood on top of this darkened basement filled with scrap lumber, rubbish, and pieces of parchment that just *might* have God's Name written on them. He thought, Maybe that's all the world stands on, too: a scrap of something with the barely legible letters of the Name of God written on it. Lose that and the whole edifice collapses.

"Is everything all right? Can you hear me?" Moshe called into the darkness.

"My hearing is fine, Señor de Guadalajara; there is no need to shout. Please be patient." And, after only a few more minutes: "Yes. Here it is. . . ."

He handed two scrolls and several more fragments up the ladder into the eager hands of the young Kabbalist. Moshe helped the old man up. They sat at the table.

"It was too dark down there to tell one from another, so I just brought everything from the bin. May I ask why this is so important to you?"

"Well, sometimes I am working very hard on an idea, but no matter how hard I work, the idea remains incomplete, unable to stand on its own, a bird missing a wing. And then one day, from out of nowhere, I stumble upon something that completes the thought. It is as if I have been looking for it, only I did not know, and it has been looking for me, *but it knew*. Well, this scrap with these phrases *botzina d'qardinuta* and *alma d'ah-tay* on it I think may be the missing wing. I am not certain, but I think that what it says—in the most economical and potent way—is the key to what I am trying to express. It is as if I wrote it to myself many years ago. May I borrow it, please?"

"Borrow it? Do not insult me; you may keep it."

"Oh, no, I couldn't, really. It must be very ancient. It must be valuable. It belongs here."

"Not at all. It is yours. Keep it, please—Don Moshe, a missing wing with your name on it."

MANHATTAN

In a dim, inchoate way, known mainly by lovers and even then recognized only in retrospect (when it is usually too late), perhaps as early as their cab ride home, but certainly now, a few days later, when they met for dinner, Kalman and Isabel each (and for different reasons) understood that what had happened in the observatory on the roof of Pupin Hall had been a mistake. They were having dinner at a Basque restaurant near the

UN. Outside there was a raw December drizzle that left a thin layer of slush capable of recording footprints for a second or two before it turned to water.

After some perfunctory small talk, Isabel said abruptly, "About the other night on the roof . . ."

"It was beautiful," he said chivalrously.

"No, it was not, Kalman. It was a *bad* idea." She hoped candor might salvage her dignity.

"But Isabel, you are one of the most . . . known . . . interesting women I have ever known. . . ."

"It's all right, Kalman. I take full responsibility. It was *I* who seduced *you*. But it was still a bad idea. Oh, Kalman, you seemed so lonely. I was hoping—"

"Stop. It's not you, Isabel. Don't you understand? It's me."

"I thought that somehow, by giving myself to you, I might help you to do the same in return. But it did not work. And don't lie, we *both* knew it in the taxicab. For once in my life, I was *too* impetuous."

"No, you weren't. It's just that I am afraid of . . ."

"Loving someone again?"

He did not say anything for a long time. "Oh, oh . . . Can't do . . . Sorry, am I . . . It's not you, Isabel. It is not you. . . ."

But she knew that, too.

"May I still call you?"

Her face was made of marble. "I think I need some space for now," she said.

They did not finish their dinners. He paid the check, and they walked over to First Avenue, where he hailed her a taxi.

The rain had turned to sleet.

· · ·

Where once her newfound courage seemed to hint at happiness, Isabel now stood waiting in line to open a charge account at the local video store. How could I have been such a fool? she thought on her way home.

Isabel did not return Kalman's calls, nor did she acknowledge his gift of a dozen more long-stemmed yellow roses. And the next week, when she had to fly down to the Caribbean for a professional meeting, she did not tell him she was leaving.

Without Isabel, Kalman's ghosts returned: He was a failure in the academy—over two decades and no dissertation. He was a failure as a congregational rabbi—a string of small, part-time pulpits. He was a failure at marriage. He was a failure at romance. He was even a failure as a mystic. The closest he came to anything authentically mystical was the damn Page with *his name on it*. He looked out the window of his office at the big red Tower Records sign across the street and tried unsuccessfully to swallow the lump in his throat.

"That's what I get for listening to Slomovitz . . . dumb Litvak."

CASTILE

The señora bade her husband, Don Judah, a safe and speedy journey to Toledo. She walked upstairs to her chamber, watching for a few minutes from the window until his carriage was out of sight. A sparrow alighted on the sill, pecked at its feathers, then flew off. She sat before her mirror to comb her hair. Still strikingly handsome, the woman she saw in the glass this morning was also undeniably old. To be sure, the señora had long understood that, like the matriarchs of old, God in His infinite wisdom had shut her womb. But *this* morning, she also knew that, after well over three decades of supplication and countless gifts to charity, *unlike* the matriarchs of old, God was not going to heed her plea: She would never bear a child.

The time of hoping and dreaming was done. She feared for a moment that she might actually die of sadness right there. Her wail could be heard throughout the house. Her maid rushed into her room only to be waved away. But before she could exit, the señora said, "Sophia, I want you to send a messenger to Don Moshe: Tell him that I shall not learn Hebrew from him today."

"Yes, ma'am."

"No, wait. I have changed my mind." She wiped her face and regained some composure. "I *shall* learn with him, but tell him that we shall learn *here*, at the summer house."

"Yes, madam."

"And Sophia, have José tell him to bring the manuscript of that book of his; I want to see it for myself."

"Yes, ma'am. Does Don Moshe's book have a name?"

"He will know which one, Sophia. Thank you."

"Señora, is anything wrong?"

"Do not worry, Sophia, I am fine. It's only from knowing that Don Judah will be gone for several days that I am sad."

"Of course, madam."

When Don Moshe arrived that afternoon, he was shown

into the library, where he could have easily occupied himself for another decade. It wasn't until he found what he suspected might be a significantly different manuscript of *Sefer ha-Bahir, The Book of Illumination,* an anonymous twelfth-century proto-Kabbalistic text, that his student appeared in the doorway. He had never been so close to a woman dressed in such elegance. Instead of her customary afternoon wardrobe, she was attired in regal splendor. Around her neck she wore a necklace of precious stones, in her hair a diadem. He had long been aware that she was handsome, but now, her face backlit by the afternoon sun—she was arrestingly beautiful. If the *Shekhina,* the Matrona, the *sefira* of the feminine indwelling divine Presence, could assume a human form (which is supposed to be unthinkable among the Jews), surely this was it. He instinctively straightened his jacket and bowed.

"Señora. Forgive me. I see that I have come at the wrong time."

"No, no, Don Moshe, I have been expecting you." Then, acknowledging her gown: "Oh, this?" she said matter-of-factly. "I had to entertain a relative of the king. Don Judah is in Toledo for two weeks' time."

Moshe nodded and helped her with her chair. He opened his valise and began placing its contents before them on the table.

"Last week we learned the grammar of irregular verbs of the *pey yod* category. . . ." If the teacher was distracted by his student, the student was even more distracted by the teacher. Her gaze was intense. He was aware, for the first time, how, when she was interested, one eyebrow raised higher than the other. To be sure, the transcript of their lesson was ordinary, even boring. . . .

LIVORNO

Harvard sociobiologist Edmund O. Wilson once wryly suggested that a human being is one gene's way of making another. In the same way, you might also say that a human being is a book's way of getting from one generation to the next. In this case, it was a nearsighted young woman named Devorah, who was the youngest granddaughter of David Cassuto of Leghorn.

As fate would have it, God, may His great Name be blessed forever and ever, had seen fit to bestow on Signor Cassuto eleven grandchildren—all girls. By number seven, he understood that God might be trying to tell him something, and by number eleven, Cassuto had, as they say, gotten the message. He chose the youngest and set about transmitting to her a love of secrets and sacred words that would be a prerequisite for inheriting the most favored books in his library.

"Can you keep a secret?" he asked little six-year-old Devorah one Sabbath afternoon. Her eyes opened wide. He sat her in his lap at the table and opened a book. "Isn't it beautiful?"

She nodded.

"Are your hands clean? Would you like to feel the page?"

He gently held her little wrist and guided her hand across the text.

"Grandfather," she said, "can you read these words?"

"Yes, little ducky, I can. And do you know what, Devorah?"

"What, Grandfather?"

"You can, too. But first, first you must learn how to pronounce them." And, pointing to a letter, he said, "This is *aleph*. Do you see how it has two feet and a little girl riding on his shoulders? He is so busy carrying that little girl, he never makes a sound. So, when you meet Mister *Aleph*..." He craned his neck so she could see his face and held an index finger up to his lips. The little girl nodded and did the same.

"Mister *Aleph*," she repeated slowly, "he is too busy carrying that little girl to make a sound...."

Their families wept tears of pride and sadness. A son, whom Rabbino Ovadya himself said should learn from the Kabbalists in the holy city of Safed, and his new bride, Devorah, bought passage on a ship bound for the Palestinian port of Yafo and what they prayed would be a life of piety and love.

And that was how the original three volumes of David Cassuto's Zohar wound up in Safed.

Safed, in northern Israel, is easily the most mystical village in the Judaic world. It is perched on such a steep mountain, they recently built an elevator there. You enter—believe it or not—from the back of the supermarket. Just ask anyone on the street. It's the ride of a lifetime: It traverses only six floors, but *five centuries*. There's no operator. Most, it must be assumed, quit halfway through their first day on the job. On the top level, there's a modern Israeli street, complete with an

ATM machine, pizzeria, and one-hour photo shop. On the bottom, you have buildings from the sixteenth century where the likes of Joseph Karo, author of the *Shulkhan Arukh*—the definitive code of Jewish law—and Shlomo Alkabetz, composer of the great Sabbath hymn "Lekha Dodi" ("Come, My Beloved"), and Isaac Luria, progenitor of Lurianic Kabbalah, studied, wrote, and prayed.

It is also probably relevant to mention here that Rabbi Shimon bar Yohai, the great second-century mystic whom Castilian Kabbalist Moshe de Leon identified as the author of the Zohar manuscript he claimed to have found, and who might even reasonably be called the protagonist of de Leon's mystical novel, is buried in Meron, about six miles up the road from the Galilean village of Safed.

MANHATTAN

One week before finals and the end of the fall semester, Kalman found himself at the library's circulation desk. It was snowing outside. "Alex in today?" he said to the young woman behind the counter.

"I saw him go up to the stacks, Rabbi Stern. Here, I'll buzz you through."

Kalman found Wasserhardt in one of the back aisles, leaning over a book cart, squinting in the dim light to read the call numbers on a volume. Kalman flipped on the light switch. "No wonder your eyesight is so bad!"

Wasserhardt looked up, startled. "Rabbi Stern, what brings you? Wait, don't tell me: Another book fell apart."

"Well, something like that . . ."

"Uh-oh, something is wrong, isn't it."

Kalman nodded. "Alex, you remember that astronomer I told you about several weeks ago?"

"The lady up at Columbia? The one you were so excited about?"

"It's over."

"She left you?"

"No, it was mutual."

"Let me understand: You like her, but you're letting her go? She's just another nice pair of legs."

"I did *not* say that. . . ."

The old man set down his book, walked over to one of the empty carrels along the wall, and sat down with a sigh. Kalman took a chair and joined him at the little desk as if he were applying for a bank loan.

"Let me tell you a story," said Wasserhardt. "I don't think I ever told it to anyone. My uncle, he was a big-time Hasid, a tailor who lived in Poland. After my bar mitzvah in Berlin, my parents sent me to spend summers with him for a few years. They thought it would be good for me to spend some time in the country. My uncle's house was near the town of Przysucha. After he'd been married for only a year or so, his wife died. They had no children, and my uncle insisted on living alone. I would help him in the shop.

"On *Shabbos*, instead of the local synagogue, we would go to his rebbe's. There, they always had a big crowd, lots of commotion—Hasidim arriving from all over by train, wagon, on foot. The praying was fervent, passionate, and ecstatic. Sometimes, when it was over, we were so exhausted we just slept on the floor. But the highlight was on Saturday afternoon around twilight. That's when the rebbe would say Torah. Everyone would cram into the big room. The old ones—they sat up in the front. We younger ones had to stand in the back. Even as a kid I could sense an urgency, a great yearning, as all those men stood singing and swaying. You could forget who you were."

"Why are you telling me all this, Alex?"

"*Sha!* When I'm done, if you want, you could ask me again, but not now. Now, where was I?"

"Something about the singing . . ."

"*Jah!* That's right. So, then the rebbe would come out and the room would grow silent. The rebbe would sit down at a table. No one made a peep. He would look off into the distance. He would say maybe a verse from the weekly *parasha*, or he would quote something from the midrash. And then he would ask this real innocent question. 'There's something I don't quite understand. How can the Torah say one thing here and another there?' And we would nod in agreement. Why, yes, that was indeed a real problem in the text. I mean, if God is the source of all sacred literature, then any contradiction must be due solely to our intellectual deficiencies. That's what a rebbe does, he helps you sharpen the apparent contradictions and then find their concealed resolution. It's all predicated, you know, on the idea that everything comes from God. And if everything comes from one source, then once it must have all fit together.

"People don't think like that much anymore. It was very exciting. But when I returned home, my parents dismissed these teachings as mere superstition unbefitting an enlightened Western Jew. Once, I remember, my father noticed I was swaying back and forth during the singing of a hymn. 'We don't do that here,' he scolded. And I never did it again. That winter my uncle died of pneumonia. You know," Wasserhardt reflected, "there aren't so many people around anymore who have had a firsthand experience of a rebbe's *tish* in Poland."

"Was he really that smart?" Kalman asked.

"Yes. That's why I'm telling you this story. You know, it's been over sixty years, and I can still remember some of his teachings. Everyone had unquestioning faith in the rebbe's ability to see into the heart of things. Some said he was like the Holy Ari himself, able to see through a man's forehead into his past and future lives. One old guy, a sweet but very simple man, went to see the rebbe with a problem, but he kept his hat pulled way down over his forehead. Afterwards, when they asked him why, he said he was afraid the rebbe would look through this forehead. 'Dummy,' they laughed, 'if he can see through your forehead, what makes you think he cannot see through your hat, too?' It was a big joke."

"He must've learned with extraordinary teachers," said Kalman.

"Oh, *jah*, but there's more. I know this will probably sound crazy, but I think they believed that the rebbe's intellectual and spiritual vision had something to do with his sexuality."

"What are you saying?"

"Of course, no one would dare utter such a thing outright, but it was understood that he was married young, very young—and everyone understood this meant that the man had never, you know, masturbated. The Hasidim believed that a man must never look lustfully at any woman except his wife and concluded that misdirected sexuality erodes the power of spiritual vision."

"I don't know about you," Kalman said (unconsciously cleaning his glasses), "but I don't think I would ever make it as a rebbe."

Both men laughed. Whereupon the old man said, "That's why it's so important to have a woman to . . . to . . ."

"Give yourself to. Yes, I know. Go ahead, say it."

Wasserhardt smiled. "*Jah*, to give yourself to."

"Alex, I'm sorry. I have tried more than once, but I can't do it."

"I believe you believe that."

"Alex, it's been two decades. I know myself. I'll be all right."

"You came up here to tell me you'll be okay? No, I don't think so. That's why I told you the story."

After a short time Kalman said, "Alex, you know that extra page in the Zohar?"

Wasserhardt nodded.

"It's talking about this, isn't it."

· Six ·

BOSTON

Judaism is a religion of books. The entire tradition is initiated by a novel: At Mount Sinai, God hands the runaway slaves (who are about to become Jews but don't know it yet) what will come to be known as the Five Books of Moses. "Here," says God, "take this home and read it. And yes, of course, you're in it. It's all about you and me. That's why I'm so eager to hear your reactions." And what the Jews think about the divine novel of which they are the protagonists is the closest they come to an indigenous theology—which is why they call Jews "the People of the Book." That is also what distinguishes Jewish fundamentalism. The Jews, assuming the words of the Torah are divine, are convinced that each word issuing from the Source of Meaning must obviously contain an *infinity* of meanings. And in this way, the Zohar—itself a novel masquerading as a commentary on God's novel—becomes inexhaustible.

Once, when his parents still lived in the old house in Dorchester, after a dutiful monthly *Shabbos* lunch, Kalman wandered downstairs to the basement and rummaged around in the detritus of his childhood. Somewhere in that mess of outgrown toys, broken appliances, and junk just might be the missing clue to whom he had become.

He was delighted but surprised when his father followed him downstairs. Together they surveyed the big bookshelf that Kalman remembered watching *him* build. And there— so thin that it was almost invisible between two other books, without even a spine, only a sheaf of printed pages and pictures between two delaminating covers—his father reverently pulled out the remains of a children's book. The name on the cover was *Boniface the Bunny*.

"Was it yours?" he asked his father.

But the old man only looked at him in surprise. "No," he said. "Don't you remember?"

"Remember what?"

"You made me read this to you over and over again before you'd go to sleep. Why, I think I had it memorized." Whereupon Kalman's father handed him the book and, to Kalman's astonishment, proceeded to recite the first few pages from memory.

But Kalman had no recollection of the story whatsoever. All that love, all those evenings—vanished.

And so it was that in this way, Kalman learned that merely finding a book is no guarantee that you will understand what it means unless there is also someone there who read it to you when you were very young and who may, indeed, have it memorized.

There is at least one such book for every person.

MANHATTAN

"REINAFIDANQUE?"

"REINAFIDANQUE." Alex spelled it out in Hebrew characters. "That's what it says. Rivkin's friend said he was pretty sure he got every letter. Why don't you come down and see for yourself?"

Kalman didn't even close his office door behind him.

"Here," Wasserhardt said, handing him the Express Mail package with the original page and Captain Ultraviolet's photographs. "My friend even printed out the letters. He must think that we can't read Hebrew. Go figure. *Resh, yod, nun, aleph, fey, yod, dalet, nun, qof,* and *yod*: ten letters."

"REINAFIDANQUE?" Kalman wrinkled his brow. "After all this time, and all Captain Ultraviolet—"

"Captain Ultraviolet? Of what is he a captain?"

"Like a comic book superhero."

"A what?"

"Never mind, Alex. I'm just disappointed that after waiting so long, all we get is gibberish."

"It certainly looks to me like gibberish. Before you came in today, I already showed it to Professor Bucholder and to Dr. Davis. They don't know what to make of it, either. It's not Hebrew or Aramaic. It's not Spanish or even Castilian— Davis, he knows some Castilian. Nothing."

"How 'bout Feldman? Did you show it to him?"

"Nothing. I'm sorry. Rivkin did ask me if you could maybe bring in the whole book sometime."

"Why?"

"He thought just in case there was something else we missed."

"Like what?"

"If I knew what it was, then we wouldn't have missed it."

"What floor is his office on in the Chrysler Building?"

"How should I know this?" Wasserhardt thumbed through his stack of business cards, pulled one out, and copied out Rivkin's phone number and address on the back of a library call slip. Then he said, "Tuesdays. Rivkin comes in then, on Tuesdays—late in the afternoons."

"Okay, okay, I'll try to stop by."

"I'm sorry, Kalman, that I couldn't get for you more information," said Alex.

"Well," said Kalman, "at least I can probably work it into a lecture." But he felt like crying.

Kalman walked back up the stairs for his coat and bag. Passing through shelves of books on medieval Europe and the

Holocaust, he noticed a red-haired young woman waiting out in front of his office. It took him a moment to recognize her.

"Hello, Rabbi Stern," she said. "I *had* to stop by and tell you in person that I just met with the admissions committee and have been accepted into the rabbinic program."

"Oh, that's really wonderful!" Kalman beamed. "Congratulations, mazel tov! Although I must confess I'm not very surprised." He unlocked the door. "Please, won't you come in? Tell me how your interview went."

"I told them all about your 1647 Livorno Zohar."

His countenance faded.

"What's the matter? Is everything okay?"

"Actually, back in September, right after you left, I discovered a letter glued inside the back cover of the Zohar, and this afternoon, I just received the final lab results. I was hoping for some more information that, alas, apparently, is not there. Here," he said, handing her the photocopy of Captain Ultraviolet's page and his translation. "See for yourself."

REINAFIDANQUE

I understand now. The botzina d'qardinuta *is the seed point of beginning, and the* alma d'ah-tay *is the mother-womb of being. Botzina d'qardinuta, it is the flash of light. Alma d'ah-tay, it is the unattainable and ultimate womb. But these two must become one. You are the darkness; I am the spark. Botzina d'qardinuta and alma d'ah-tay.*

Moshe ben Shem Tov de Guadalajara

"What is REINAFIDANQUE?" she said, looking up.

"I wish I knew, too. Experts have tried everything—but no luck."

"How about *botzina d'qardinuta* and *alma d'ah-tay*? What do they mean?"

"*Botzina d'qardinuta* means a spark containing within itself all subsequent creation. It corresponds to the second *sefira* of *Hokhma*, or insight. And *alma d'ah-tay* literally means the world that is coming and corresponds to the third *sefira* of *Bina*, or intuition. She is the mother of being. But the author," said Kalman, "and he's who we were hoping to learn more about, also seems to be describing how they also correspond to him and his lover."

"What if the author of the Zohar wrote them himself?" she said, unable to conceal her own enthusiasm.

"That was the big hunch. We do know that Moshe de Leon was originally from Guadalajara. It's a definite possibility."

"Rabbi Stern," she said, "the letter is describing what happens in every loving relationship: The lovers must permit themselves to dissolve into each other. You know, the love you have is the love you give."

"But don't you think it is equally important for the lovers to remain discrete and independent from each other?"

"Sure, but without ultimately relinquishing their separateness, their love is a sham."

"A sham!?" said Kalman, startled.

"Well, maybe not a sham, but, you know, from the outside it appears like loving, but it is incomplete."

Kalman wished he could tell Isabel what the young

woman had said. He was surprised by how sad it made him feel that he could not. So instead he said, "You will make a fine rabbi; you are a very wise young woman."

She smiled. "I have a *very* loving husband."

"He's also a fortunate man."

"You know," she said, "I think this might be a reason mystics are so commonly drawn to erotic imagery. Like lovers, they believe that in order to *find* themselves, they must *lose* themselves."

(He wished he could take notes.) "So, you'll be going to Israel this summer with the first-year class?"

"We're so excited."

"There's a magical little synagogue I hope you'll visit up in Safed. . . ."

CASTILE

"It makes no sense," said Don Moshe. "I understand the first part: You are saying that from the Nothingness of the *Ayn Sof*, there emerges a dark spark. But this spark is too faint to have any effect or even to be visible. And that only once it is received within the fecund reflection of *Bina* can its seminal radiance generate the seven lower *sefirot*, the seven days of the week, and, finally, this, our sublunar world. Up to there I understand what you are saying. But then you say that in order for this to happen, the spark must completely *give itself away*, relinquish its very identity, just as a woman's womb must receive the light so completely that she too can no longer remain who she was. The borders of each, in other words, must dissolve before they can each be realized. It makes no sense. How by relinquishing itself, and permitting its own dissolution, could there come redemption, fulfillment, and apotheosis?"

"Don Moshe, you do not understand because you are talking like a philosopher and not a Kabbalist," said the señora. "Of course *according to logic* something cannot dissolve itself and realize itself simultaneously. But, Don de Guadalajara, *according to life*, yes. I know this happens."

Moshe looked at his pupil as if she had just told him the *raza d'razin*—the secret of existence (which in fact, of course, she just had). "That would mean that creation is not a point in space and time, but potentially everywhere and all the time. And every dissolution is also a creation. . . ."

"You see, you *do* understand. Creation is continuously happening. There is no single point of beginning."

"And all the *sefirot*, they all happen at once?!"

"And why not?" she said.

"That would mean that we can enter them all, that we can reexperience the moment of creation whenever we choose. It is not long ago; it is now!" As Moshe spoke these words, it seemed to him as if he had said something that was simultaneously holy and dangerous. A fleeting but oblique glance toward her revealed the same fear and reverence—too dangerous to acknowledge, too beautiful to ignore.

That shared glance was the closest they ever came to physical intimacy.

"A seed spark that is not yet light and a womb containing only the possibility of the world yet to come. How would you say that, Don Moshe?"

He shrugged. "I do not know, señora. I do not know what it would be. . . ."

That evening, long after their lesson and after dinner, Don Moshe ben Shem Tov de Guadalajara climbed the stairs to his room. "She is the teacher," he said aloud to himself, "and I am *her* student."

He sat in silence, watching the shadows fill the room. When it grew too dark to read his notes, Moshe cleaned the wick of the small oil lamp, opened his tinderbox, and struck the flint on the stone. There was a tiny bit of light, barely a spark, more dark than light, not even enough to ignite the tinder. A smile formed on his lips and he whispered, "A seed of darkened light planted within the womb of all being yet to come. Of course! How could I have not seen it before!"

He hurried to open his satchel and remove a sheet of paper. He sharpened a quill, opened a small bottle of ink, and wrote: "Now I understand. *Botzina d'qardinuta* is the seed point of beginning, and the *alma d'ah-tay* is the mother-womb of being. *Botzina d'qardinuta*, he is the flash of light. *Alma d'ah-tay*, she is the unattainable and ultimate womb. But these two must become one. You are the darkness; I am the spark. *Botzina d'qardinuta* and *alma d'ah-tay*." He addressed it and signed his name.

And as he did, he saw her face before him. Because of her, he now understood that these two phrases, *botzina d'qardinuta* and *alma d'ah-tay*, had been vouchsafed unto him. Because of her, these phrases had now made him into their vessel. Something new and wonderful could be born. His book was *her* child. And it seemed to him at that moment that God's purpose in creating the world was solely that he, Moshe ben Shem Tov, might write these words on this paper and transmit them into the hands of his extraordinary student. God, in His infinite wisdom, had intended that she should be his student. God had intended that she should be his teacher. From their very first lesson until the extraordinary discovery of this evening, nothing had been happenstance. Somehow her wisdom and, yes, her beauty had made his discovery possible. He uttered a verse from the Song of Songs: "*Libav-tini b'ahat may-ae-naiykh*—You have stolen my heart with one glance. . . ."

The sound of a donkey cart rattling past his window startled him. He looked at the quill in his hand; he looked down at the words on the page; he understood that obviously he must have written them. But for the life of him, he could not remember doing so. The words seemed to have been written by a hand other than his own. But wherever they came from, the words were too important to wait the week until his next meeting with the señora; they had to be shared at once. He walked out to the stable and roused one of the boys.

"In Valladolid, do you know the walled mansion overlooking the plaza, the one by the big water trough? There are red and white roses in the front. . . . Excellent. One dinero is yours if you take this letter to his wife tomorrow morning. Do not give it to a servant. Do you understand?"

How could he possibly have foreseen that Don Judah, assuming that any such urgent communication must obviously be for him, would not bother to read the address and open it himself instead?

MANHATTAN

Kalman slid his MetroCard through the turnstile reader and walked down the long ramp of the West Fourth Street subway station. From there he would be able to take the uptown express. An old black man in a fedora was singing the blues and accompanying himself on a guitar, an upturned hat on the pavement in front of him. A young mother was trying to persuade the screaming infant on her hip to take a bottle. And a Latino couple was locked in a passionate embrace; no one paid them any notice. Little black dots that used to be chewing gum littered the pavement. When they talk about melting pots, they mean the West Fourth Street subway station, thought Kalman. He made his way toward the end of the platform, hoping to board an empty car on the train. But instead Kalman found Milton Slomovitz.

"Milt!" he said.

"Stern, what are you doing here? I thought mystics didn't need the subway." He waved one of his hands as if it were a bird in flight.

"Sometimes I like to see how the hoi polloi get around."

"Of course." Slomovitz smiled. "I understand. I'll keep it in the strictest of confidence."

And then, in the universal manner of people waiting for a subway, they leaned over the platform's edge and peered into the tunnel, hoping to see the headlight of an oncoming train.

"Speaking of getting around, I read that there's a tenured position opening up in medieval history and philosophy out at UCLA."

"Milton Slomovitz in Southern California? Surely you jest."

"Hey, Kal, it can't hurt to look."

"What about the smog and the earthquakes and Sheila's husband, what was his name? Harvey? I thought you couldn't—"

"They're getting a divorce."

"My God, you're serious, aren't you."

"It'll probably come to nothing."

Kalman looked at him. "Milt, I do believe I would actually miss you."

"I would miss you, too, you crazy mystic. But at least you would still have your astronomer."

Kalman did not reply.

"She dumped you, didn't she."

"Let's just say we had different visions of what our relationship was supposed to become."

"You want I should break her kneecaps?"

Kalman did not smile. "What I want is to stop getting so emotionally involved with women."

"I'm sorry, Kal. Well, at least you still have your mystery page. Any word yet from Captain Ultraviolet at Oxford?"

Kalman's expression relaxed. "As a matter of fact, Wasserhardt got it back a couple days ago. I was going to call."

"And . . . ?"

"Zip. We are now able to read the entire erasure, but as far as anyone can tell, it's only a meaningless string of letters. *REINAFID* . . . something. Gibberish."

"Such a shame after all that effort. I would still like to see it sometime."

"You can see a photocopy right now, if you like." Kalman opened his pack and produced the ultraviolet photograph. "See what I mean?" he said, pointing to the top. "It's definitely not Hebrew or Aramaic or Arabic. Bucholder can't figure it out, neither can Davis—and he knows *all* those languages. I've even tried gematria. It adds up to 506—nothing! I'm flat out of strategies. As far as I can tell, it's just a string of letters."

Slomovitz looked down at the piece of paper for a minute and then back at Kalman. "The reason you can't translate it is because it's *not* a word; it's a name."

"Someone named Reinafidanque?" Kalman knotted his brow. "What kind of name is that?"

"I didn't say it was *one* name. It's two. You need to put a space after the first *a*. Reina Fidanque."

"But on a page of Kabbalistic notes written by Moshe de Guadalajara?"

"Why not? Isn't that what all you crazy mystics like so much about names anyway? They're like mystical experiences—beyond language. Wasn't it Walter Benjamin, yes, I'm sure it was Walter Benjamin, who said that names are the least semantic function of language; they're literally meaningless sounds. Yet the name carries the essence of the person."

"But who was he?"

"Well, for openers, he is definitely *not* a man. *She* is a woman."

"A woman . . ."

"Yes, Reina. It was not an uncommon name among Spanish women, and if memory serves me, Fidanque was the name of a prominent Jewish family. Around the time of the expulsion, they went underground—you know, Marranos, Conversos. I seem to remember that it showed up again in Holland, an influential commercial family. That's where, you know, a lot of them fled, Holland."

"But why would a fourteenth-century Spanish Kabbalist write a woman's name on the top of a page of . . . My God, Milton, this means it really could be a letter!"

"Maybe he knew her," Slomovitz said. "Maybe she was his friend." And then, with a wink: "Maybe she was his mistress."

"No!"

"What's the matter, you don't think Kabbalists can fall in love? Maybe your Kabbalist was in love with a woman named Reina Fidanque and he wrote her a love letter."

Kalman just stared at the Page.

He didn't even hear the A train roaring out of the tunnel.

SAFED: SIXTH ITERATION

The old man walked over to an alcove in the center of the side wall of the synagogue. The alcove was up one step and was covered by a maroon velvet curtain decorated with gold ornaments and tassels. Behind the curtain were two tall mahogany doors. And then, as if he were removing a coffeemaker from the kitchen cupboard, he took out a long brass tube attached to a collapsed tripod.

"You want to give me a hand with this thing? It's heavy."

Kalman took the other end of the tube—it had an eye-piece on one end. "Why is there a telescope in the ark?"

"Beats me," said the old man. "I just found it there myself; one day I opened the holy ark, and instead of a Torah scroll, there was this long brass tube. But wait till you look *through* it."

Together the two men maneuvered the contraption over to the windows. The caretaker adjusted the tripod. "With this, you could see the color of God's eyes—that is, if God had eyes." The light streaming in through the window was very bright. "Here, give a look-see."

Kalman removed his glasses and lowered his eye to the lens. He saw a huge red neon triangle on a white neon back-ground with big blue letters across the bottom. "Hey, that's the Citgo sign in Kenmore Square! It's in Boston! I grew up in Boston!"

"Great city, Boston. But try to relax. Take a few deep breaths." The old man carefully adjusted a few of the knobs and motioned for Kalman to have another look.

This time Kalman saw a slightly overweight adolescent boy looking through the nine-inch Alvan Clark refractor tel-escope on the rooftop of a Harvard building in Cambridge, Massachusetts. "Why, that's me!"

"Who'd you expect?"

"But that was over thirty years ago!"

"Everything happens at once. You want to see further?"

"Further? You mean I can see even more of the past?"

"Uh-huh. Here, try this knob." The mechanism felt old, unused, like rubbing stones together.

This time Kalman saw a field on a sunny afternoon. A man and a woman, in Middle Ages clothing, were having a picnic. She was finishing an orange, and the man was writing with a quill pen on a piece of paper. "I can't make out what they're saying," said Kalman.

"May I give a try?"

Kalman stepped back.

Squinting through the lens, the old man said, "You speak Castilian?"

"No."

"That's why you can't understand them; they're speaking Old Castilian."

"Old Castilian? What are they saying?"

"Shhh. Let me listen. . . . Ah, yes. The woman just said, 'Adam, if you are still listening, I did not mean the words I spoke only moments ago. Go right ahead; eat of the fruit.'"

Kalman said, "That's what Eve says to Adam! But she's speaking in Spanish, and it looks like they're in the Middle Ages."

"If you could exceed the speed of light and you had a good enough telescope, you could watch everything that has ever happened or everything that ever will," said the caretaker.

"But you'd have to be at the event horizon of the universe."

"That's right. The event horizon is not somewhere *out* there; it is homogenously distributed throughout all creation.

In principle, you can see anything from anywhere. It's everywhere. It's in this room. In me. In you."

"You can see the future, too?"

"Why not? Adam could."

"I beg your pardon?"

"Adam could see the future—at least until he sinned and brought division into the world. It has to do with the connection between human behavior and awareness—just like it says at the beginning of the Zohar. He and Eve had ultimate consciousness until God realized that they'd use it to make a mess of things."

"Oh, I understand: Morality and vision are related. The better you are, the more you see. The more you see, the better you are."

"Amazing, isn't it? You can see every sin that has ever been or ever will be committed. You can watch them while they happen."

"That means that everything is always happening and you can always watch it," said Kalman. He leaned over the eyepiece again. "Where did she go?"

"Who?"

"The woman, the one speaking Spanish."

"You must've bumped the eyepiece. Remember, this thing is very, very sensitive. With even the slightest touch, you can move hundreds of miles and years—even decades." The old man fiddled with the focus. "Wait, I think I've got him again. . . . Yes, here he is. Just be careful; don't move the lens."

Kalman looked again. "Yes, that's him. But now he's at a table writing something. Now he's sealing it. It must be a letter. My God, this could really become addictive—especially if you knew how to aim it. I mean, how do you know exactly where to look?"

"As far as I can tell," replied the caretaker, "you can look anywhere. It's all covered in the instruction manual."

"Instruction manual?"

"Yes. Let me see. It's here somewhere." The old man walked over to a pile of books in the corner and, after rejecting two or three, selected one. He blew off the dust and began thumbing through its pages as if he knew just what he was looking for. "Yes, yes. Here it is." He tilted the open book so that Kalman could make out what looked like a chart, a page of columned numbers, coordinates. "Invaluable, absolutely invaluable," he whispered to Kalman.

"Amazing, simply amazing."

"Here, you take it. It's yours—has your name on it."

POLAND

"You knew Zeitman!?"

"Knew him? I was with him when he died. His death is probably the reason *I'm* still here," said Dovid Rivkin, the paleographer and friend of Captain Ultraviolet.

That got Kalman's attention. He forgot all about the 1647 Livorno Zohar with its extra page, which until a moment ago he had thought was the reason for his visit.

Rivkin's office made Kalman's look neat. It was filled with

old books and papers and a lot of dust. Its bookshelves and file cabinets had long ago been supplanted by three- and four-foot-high stacks along three walls. There was a calendar on the wall for 1993.

"I was going to write a doctoral dissertation on Zeitman. I must have read everything the man has ever written," said Kalman.

Rivkin was easily in his late seventies. But he looked even older. He was one of those men, Kalman imagined, who probably looked like an old man when he was a teenager. The mention of the name Zeitman seemed to have triggered a distant memory.

"The odor was horrible. Human waste, the stench of rotting flesh. Some of the passengers on the train were near catatonic, others hysterical. Most of us were simply beyond fear or feeling. I wound up sitting on the floor next to this old man who, despite the chaos, seemed deep in thought. He told me his name was Aaron Zeitman. And I know this may be hard to believe, but he actually began talking with me as if I'd just met him on the trolley, as if nothing strange were happening at all. We talked about an article he'd written on the Zohar. I remember our conversation—everything. The woman sitting next to me on the floor must have died shortly after we boarded the train. I thought she was only asleep, but Zeitman pointed out that she had stopped breathing. Do you think it will rain tomorrow? There I was, sitting in a boxcar with one of the great Kabbalistic minds of the generation on one side and the corpse of a woman on the other. I even remember the date. It was *erev* Rosh Hashanah. I'm sure of this because Mordecai Gellner had this little shofar. Don't ask me why he had it. This evening, you'll be going on a one-way trip to hell; is there anything perhaps you'd like to take along for the ride? Gellner took a shofar. It was very small and sounded more like the screech of the train's brakes than a ram's horn. He raised it to his lips, and Yudel gave the calls: '*Tekiah, shevarim-teruah, teruah.*' 'Remember us for life, O King, who is supposed to delight in life.' When he heard the shofar, Zeitman reached into his coat and brought out his tallis and tefillin. I remember thinking, You don't wear tefillin on *yontif.*

"Sometime in the middle of that night, the transport stopped. It was so cold I could feel the hairs inside my nose. We could hear the soldiers walking alongside the transport and smashing open the door bolts with the butts of their guns. They spoke as if we were not there.

" 'Go on, Rudi, show them.'

" 'Show them?'

"The door of our car rolled open—a window into the night. We began moving out onto the platform.

" '*Jah*, show the vermin all about their God.'

"It was so cold I could see my breath. There must have been hundreds of us, all making little puffs of white soul-smoke. Even the soldiers made soul-smoke, just like the Jews. The puffs disappeared into the night sky.

" 'Here, show them with this.' His buddy tossed him a pistol.

"Zeitman just went on reciting the liturgy from memory, oblivious to what was happening. He looked like a *luftmensch*— a man of the heavens. I would never forget the radiance on his face. For a minute I even forgot where we were. Everything stopped. He said, 'I am going to die, but you are not. Here, I want you to have this.' "

"Have what?" whispered Kalman.

"He just said two Aramaic phrases, *botzina d'qardinuta* and *alma d'ah-tay*, a flash of light and the world that is coming."

Kalman gasped. "He said that?! He said *botzina d'qardinuta* and *alma d'ah-tay*?!"

"Yes, that is what he said. He said that was how God did it."

"Did what?"

"The world. He said that that was how God made it. They were the mechanism through which the World of Unity creates this World of Separation. It's the central question of Kabbalah: How did God do it? He said they must be willing to surrender themselves to each other. Neither will ever be the same again.

"The kid was loading the gun, and we went right on talking as if we were strolling through the park. You know, Rabbi Stern, I must have thought about those words a thousand times, and I still am not sure what he meant. Even after all these years, the closest I can come is that he believed there is a place where we realize that both life *and* death are *within* God, and when you enter *that* place, you lose your fear of dying because a child is about to be born."

"Did *you* stop being afraid of dying?"

"No, I didn't. Though to tell you the truth, at the time I was more afraid I would live. I remember that the soldier was just a kid, nineteen, maybe twenty at the most. He was so eager to impress his friends. But his hand was shaking. And then, to make his own terror go away, he pulled the trigger and shot Zeitman. Just like that. He walked around behind the only man left praying in the whole world and shot him in the back of the head. Blood and brains and bone and tefillin splattered all over the side of the boxcar.

" 'Where's your God now, Jew?' said one of the soldiers.

"But the kid was white as a sheet. He had been mistaken. His terror did not go away. He walked over to the side of the platform and threw up while his buddies laughed.

"And in the commotion, I just walked off into the night. I walked through the frosted crisp stubble of some kind of field; I climbed a fence, all the while just watching the white puffs of breath coming out of my mouth. I imagined that I was a human steam locomotive chugging through the field. I was certain I would be shot at any moment. But the bullet never came. I just walked and I walked and I walked until I stumbled and fell asleep, huddled in a stack of hay. The next morning, I realized that his blood was on me, Zeitman's blood was spattered all over my clothes. And I remember what he said: 'Here, I would like you to have this.' "

"If you still remember it after all these years," said Kalman, "then I think that means you have received whatever gift it was."

"Yes, Rabbi Stern, I have thought that, too. And now, whatever it was, I suppose, belongs to you, too."

CASTILE

Early the next day, Moshe left Valladolid, heading for his home in Ávila and what promised to be a very lucrative meeting with a new buyer of Kabbalistic manuscripts from Akko. A little more than halfway into the journey, Moshe took a room for the night in the town of Arévalo. He had only just extinguished the candle when he was startled by two strangers who had somehow effortlessly opened his locked door. The shorter of the two, walking with a slight limp, lit the lamp; the taller man held his finger to his lips.

"Hush," he whispered.

Even in the dim light, Moshe could see that his face was badly pockmarked. "Who are you?" said Moshe, sitting up in his bed.

"Servants of Don Judah."

"What is the matter?"

"Everything is fine . . . fine, now that we have found *you*."

"Found me? What do you want with me? It is Don Judah's wife, isn't it. Oh, my God, something has happened to her."

"No, she is fine. She is on a journey."

"A journey!? She said nothing of a journey to me. I do not understand."

"Don Judah now understands that you have taught his wife more than Hebrew."

Moshe involuntarily glanced toward the door as the shorter stranger limped over to the exit. "I don't understand."

"Fool, did you think a man like Don Judah could be deceived so easily?"

"Deceived?"

"Listen to him: dumb and innocent," the face said to the limp. And, turning to the man in bed: "Don Judah has read your letter to his wife."

"Letter? What letter?"

"But you are fortunate. Don Judah may be very jealous of his possessions, but he is also very compassionate," continued the taller one. "He does not believe in violent retribution." At this, he slid his left hand along his belt, slowly, opening his cloak so as to reveal the scabbard of a long knife. Then he nodded to his companion, who removed a small parcel from his coat and began unwrapping what looked like a vial.

"The actual event itself"—he spoke as if he were explaining the details of a routine business contract—"will not be painful."

Moshe's heart was pounding. "What are you talking about?"

"It will happen while you are asleep." He corrected himself: "That is, it will *appear* that it happened while you were asleep. . . ."

"This is a terrible mistake. I must speak with Don Judah immediately."

"There is nothing to say. Don Judah has already read your love letter to his wife."

"My love letter? What are you talking about? Surely you

don't mean the note I gave to the stable boy, with *botzina d'qardinuta* and *alma d'ah-tay*? This is madness. I have never touched the woman. Please, I am begging you, let me speak with Don Judah."

"That will be impossible. He has left for Toledo with his wife this morning."

"But then she has not seen the letter. . . ."

"Don Judah has decided that the knowledge of your death will be sufficient punishment for her."

"My death?"

But alas, as everyone knows, when there are no options, the choice is easy. Moshe wondered how death would taste in his mouth. Would it be bitter or sweet? Would he perhaps see the *botzina d'qardinuta*, the dark spark, on his way back into the *alma d'ah-tay*—the world that is coming?

He raised the vial to his lips, surprised that his hand did not tremble, and swallowed its contents. The liquid tasted spicy, a little sweet. For decades he had been certain that his dying words would have been the declaration of God's unity. But he was mistaken. The Shema was the furthest thing from his mind. Instead he saw only her face, the joy with which she confided her thoughts, the light on her hair, her wisdom, and, so clearly now, her eyes. "*Libav-tini b'ahat may-ae-naiykh*—You have stolen my heart with one glance. . . ."

SEVEN

MANHATTAN

The Chrysler Building, on the northeast corner of Lexington and Forty-second, was completed in 1930. For a few months, until it was displaced by the Empire State, its seventy-seven floors and spire of arched stainless-steel sunbursts with triangular windows, manufactured in Germany by the Krupp Company, made it the tallest building in the world. Brooklyn architect William Van Alen drew the plans for Walter P. Chrysler, owner of Chrysler Motors, who said he wanted something that declared "the glories of the modern age." At the time of its construction, there was a big race to build the tallest skyscraper in the world. The Bank of Manhattan Building, being erected at the same time and designed to be two feet taller than the Chrysler, had apparently won. But Van Alen had been secretly assembling the stainless-steel spire in five pieces in one of the building's elevator shafts. And at the last minute, in what is surely one of the great architectural fandangos of all time, before throngs of pedestrians below, its twenty-seven tons were hoisted into place, raising the Chrysler's height to 1,046 feet, 119 feet taller than the Bank of Manhattan! There are thirty-two elevators in the Chrysler; they were built and installed by the Otis Elevator Company. And until that December, Kalman Stern had never been in one of them.

Even after carefully examining the entire Livorno Zohar volume, Rivkin was unable to add anything helpful. There were no more hidden pages, no more clues. After almost three months, Kalman had run out of leads. He was the proud owner of one volume of a 350-year-old Zohar and one much older additional page. And except for whoever Reina Fidanque was, he knew what all the words meant. It was also at least even odds that Moshe ben Shem Tov de Guadalajara was none other than Moshe de Leon, author of the Zohar. But without some kind of context for the page, it might as well have been a grocery list. On the other hand, it hadn't been a total loss. He had learned a lot about paleography and collected enough information on the manufacture of the Zohar to consider writing an essay for the *Journal of Kabbalistic Studies*. And, maybe most important of all, he had met a man who had actually talked to Aaron Zeitman and witnessed his death. Maybe he would take his two-decades-old Zeitman dissertation out of the drawer and write a new last chapter.

By the time Kalman left Dovid Rivkin's office up on the thirty-second floor of the Chrysler Building, it was past seven o'clock. Most of the other offices along the corridor were already closed, their occupants headed home for supper. Kalman took a moment to admire the industrial simplicity of the building's art deco architecture—the clean sweep of lines, the parallel curves, the burnished metal. They don't build 'em like this anymore, he thought. Lost for a moment in 1930, he even forgot he was walking toward the bank of elevators and the ordeal of yet another elevator ride. (Walking down thirty-two flights was not an option.)

So a ride in one of Elisha Graves Otis's "safety hoisters" was the only choice. He did the math in his head: thirty-two floors at approximately two seconds per floor . . . one minute of potential hell and he'd be free again. He pressed the "down" button and the doors opened. Thank God no one was inside. At least he could sweat in solitude. By contemporary standards, the elevator car itself was surprisingly small. This particular one—in the Chrysler, no two are identical—was paneled in a mosaic of three or four different-colored woods. The lighting was soft and recessed. It was a kinetic sculpture, a work of art, thought Kalman. My God, even the ceiling had a one-of-a-kind aluminum inset of a starburst. "A spark of light containing everything yet to come . . ."

Then he remembered where he was. So much for art. His pulse quickened. Taking a deep breath and exhaling slowly, he pressed "L" and tried fixing his gaze on the lighted floor number panel above the elevator's doors. He did not notice a burnished metal sign just to the right of the door and below the panel of floor buttons, informing any anxious passenger that an inspection certificate was available in the building manager's office at 666 Third Avenue on the eighteenth floor. Nor, for that matter, did he notice an even smaller brass plaque affixed to the wall just below it. That plate read:

> *Those who heal the past can redeem the present*
> OTIS ELEVATOR COMPANY

Kalman counted off the floors with each *ding*. But after the twenty-fourth *ding,* the car came to a stop. The doors opened and a woman wheeled in another woman in a wheelchair. Kalman managed a polite smile as he was wedged into the back corner of the elevator.

The woman in the wheelchair was very pregnant. The woman pushing her looked very frightened. A man stood in the hall, holding open the elevator's doors. Kalman figured he was a doctor because he wore a white coat and had a stethoscope slung around his neck. He spoke in one of those reassuring voices that reassured no one—not the very pregnant woman in the wheelchair, not the frightened woman pushing it, and certainly not Kalman: "Isadora, you're going to be just fine. And don't worry if you're a little wet; that will be what's left of the amniotic fluid. The ambulance guys will probably be at the Lexington Avenue entrance before you get there."

"Not if you don't shut up," Kalman muttered to himself.

"I'll just lock up the office, and if I don't see you downstairs,

I'll meet you at the hospital." Then the doctor said to Kalman, "We have a woman in labor here. Her water broke in my office, but not to worry. She's only dilated four centimeters; I'm confident she has several hours to go." He looked at the woman pushing the wheelchair. "Monica, you relax, too. All you have to do is get Isadora down to Lexington Avenue and the EMT boys'll do the rest. I'll be down on the next car."

Monica attempted a weak smile, whereupon the doctor reached around inside the car, pressed "L" several times, and stepped back into the corridor. As the doors closed, Monica turned to Kalman and whispered, "I'm just an agency temp."

Together, they listened to the *ding*s as they passed each floor. *Ding*, fifteen. *Ding*, fourteen. *Ding*, twelve . . . Whereupon there was a soft *pop* accompanied by a slight jerk as the elevator stopped. Then the lights went out. There was a faint smell of ozone, and the emergency battery lights clicked on with a soft buzz.

"Oh, my God," said Monica. "What's happening?" Her blouse was wet with perspiration.

"Probably just a momentary power failure," said Kalman. "Hello? Anybody . . . out there?" There was no reply. "I'm sure it'll a few minutes just be." Kalman was perspiring now, too.

"I certainly hope so."

Kalman picked up the emergency telephone receiver and dialed the number printed on the instruction card.

"Yeah," said the voice, "we know. They accidentally sliced a cable over at some construction site on Third Avenue. But hey, don't worry; we're working on it. We'll have you outta there within an hour. Say, buddy—don't go anywhere. Ha ha ha ha . . ."

"Thanks a lot."

"Is it okay?" asked the woman in the wheelchair. "Is everything okay?"

"Not to worry. The guy said they'll have the power restored in a few minutes. You don't happen to have a deck of cards, do you?"

She shook her head without smiling. Then she let out a moan.

With the air-conditioning off, the tiny cubicle quickly grew hot. Kalman folded his jacket and set it on the floor, then on top of it he placed the Livorno Zohar that had gotten him into this whole mess.

Now the woman made a much deeper, more primal noise and said, "Get me out of this goddamn chair!"

Kalman nodded and knelt to fold back the wheelchair's footrests. He was about to ask Monica to steady the contraption from the back when he realized that Monica was not listening to him. Monica was not listening to anyone. Monica was pale and perspiring. Monica was fainting. Leaning into the corner, as if she had rehearsed it for months, she slid down to the floor in a neat little heap.

So Kalman offered his arm to the woman in the chair, who helped herself up and then eased herself slowly onto the floor.

Kalman picked up the phone again, but this time there was no answer. "Do you have a cell phone?"

After fumbling in her purse, she handed it to him. He punched 911. Nothing. He punched O. Again nothing. Then he looked at the screen and saw that there were no bars. "It doesn't look like we have any reception in here," he said, handing it back.

The woman winced.

"Are you all right? What's going to happen?" Kalman said to the woman, unable to conceal his own anxiety.

"I'm going to have a baby, that's what's going to happen."

"Can I do anything to help?"

"Yes. You can turn the power back on."

"No, really."

"Really. I've never had a baby before."

"Me neither."

They both laughed. The laughter made them friends.

A moment later, she gave another moan and Kalman felt his mouth go dry. From out of the corner of his eye, he noticed that the Zohar had somehow slid out of its bubble-wrap envelope and was now lying open on the floor. In the bright emergency lights, the letters no longer looked like Hebrew characters. They appeared to him, instead, to be English. He blinked his eyes, trying to clear his vision, but they were still English. Even more important, so were the words— English words in a 1647 Zohar. This is really amazing, he thought.

The woman screamed again.

He remembered how in a movie he saw once, when a woman was having a baby and there were no clean cloths available, the man had taken off his shirt and torn it into strips. He took off his parka and sports jacket, but when he tried to open his shirt, his hands were shaking so that he couldn't undo the buttons. So he tore it off. The buttons made little popping sounds as they hit the elevator's walls.

He managed to collapse the wheelchair, then took his

jacket and folded it into a pillow for the woman's head. She seemed to draw comfort from his presence.

Just at that moment, the emergency power lights began to flicker.

"Oh, God, it's coming!"

"The darkness?"

"No, the baby!"

Kalman glanced once more at the open Zohar on the floor.

When about 3 or 4 cm of the head is visible during a contraction, the physician (if right-handed) places the left palm over the baby's head during a contraction to control and, if necessary, slightly retard its progress, while placing the curved fingers of the right hand against the dilating perineum, through which the baby's brow or chin is felt. Applying pressure against the brow or chin with curved fingers helps advance the head.

"What's the perineum?" Kalman said.

"What am I, a doctor?"

"Maybe there's a commentary," he said.

"A what?"

And sure enough, there, in the left margin, was a note anticipating the reader's question.

The perineum is the region between the posterior vulva junction and the anus in females. After delivery of the head, the baby's body rotates so that the shoulders are in an anteroposterior position; gentle downward pressure on the head delivers the anterior shoulder. . . .

Kalman rotated the child's head and pushed down ever so slightly, freeing a shoulder. He looked down at the tiny soul, expecting a moment of relief and pride, but the baby was blue. It was not breathing.

After delivery of the baby, the physician places a hand gently on the uterine fundus to detect contractions; placental separation usually occurs during the first or second contraction, often with a gush of blood from behind the separating placenta. The mother can usually assist in the delivery of the placenta by pushing. . . . The baby's nose, mouth, and pharynx are aspirated with a bulb syringe to remove mucus and fluids and help establish respiration.

"But I don't have a bulb syringe. There's nothing here I could use to . . ."

And without any conscious deliberation, as if he'd practiced it every day for years, in one quick and flawless gesture, he tore a page from the Zohar. After rolling it between his palms, he inserted the narrow tube like a soda fountain straw into the infant's tiny throat and, very gently, sucked. Whereupon, like a little lawn mower starting up after a long winter in the garage, the infant sputtered, wheezed, coughed, and finally began to breathe on its own.

Kalman glanced down at the Livorno Zohar lying open on the elevator floor. He said, "Great book, the Zohar: one thousand and one uses. Really a *great* book."

·   ·   ·

Upon hearing a woman's screams, a small crowd had assembled in the lobby. The police and the EMT ambulance were already at the Lexington Avenue entrance and behind them the media.

"Can you hear me up there?" someone called up the shaft.

"Yes. Yes, we can hear you."

"Is everything okay?"

"Yes, I think so."

"We've got some power to the cable, but all the computer settings seem to have been erased. You'll need to press a floor button to restart the car."

"The battery lights are about all gone. It's almost pitch black in here. We can't see a thing."

"Can you feel the panel?"

"I can feel the buttons."

"The first two are for the basement and the sub-basement. You want—"

"The third one," he said.

"Yes, the third one. That's right. How'd you know?"

"The third one opens the sky," said Kalman.

There was a mechanical hum and a loud *kerchunk* as the elevator resumed its earthward journey. But now it carried four passengers instead of three.

As the doors opened, those assembled saw the new mother lying on her back, holding a slippery newborn infant, and, seated cross-legged on the floor like a Buddha, a bare-chested, middle-aged, curly-haired man. Behind him, just regaining consciousness, was a second woman. All four had tears in their eyes, but each for a different reason.

.   .   .

Kalman stepped out of the elevator into a small crowd disproportionately populated with members of the press. The EMT squad almost tripped him as they rushed into the elevator with a gurney. A policeman offered him a blanket. "C'mon, folks, give the guy a break. He's had a rough couple of hours."

Kalman told the police what had happened and the reporters as little as he could without being rude. Someone helped him exchange the blanket for his sports coat and parka. "No, I'm all right, thanks. I'll be just fine," he said. "No, I don't need a shirt. Really, thank you for all your help." As he was finally about to leave the lobby, one of the policemen emerged from the elevator and called after him, "Hey, buddy, you forgot your book. . . ."

Across Lexington Avenue, in the window of an electronics store with a big permanent sign in the window that said, GOING OUT OF BUSINESS! EVERYTHING MUST GO!, Kalman caught a reflection of the entrance to the Chrysler Building. Above its entrance was a good-sized neon sign that he had never noticed before. No one had ever noticed it before. It had never been there before he noticed it. So it naturally took Kalman by surprise and a moment to read it backward in the mirror of the window. But when he did, it said, THE CHRYSLER BUILDING IS ITSELF A SIGN.

"What . . . ?" he said, turning around to corroborate the reflection in the window. But there was no sign there.

THE BOOK OF LOVE'S
FINAL FRAGMENT

It was chilly out on the street, especially with no shirt on, but Kalman barely noticed. "Hey," he consoled himself, "I just delivered a baby, I think. Or maybe this is what it means when they say Kabbalah can make you crazy." He unzipped his parka and stuffed his cap into a side pocket. Then he glanced over his shoulder at the Chrysler Building one last time before walking down into the subway station. Once there, he found only three people on the platform. "Just missed one, damn." On the other hand, at least there was an open bench. He plugged the jack into his Walkman, inserted the ear bud into his ear, and tapped "play." It was Artie Shaw. Nonchalantly, hoping not to attract attention, he reached into his bag. He wanted to touch the envelope that held the old book and his credentials as a bona fide mystic. "It's all mine," he said to Artie Shaw, who just kept on playing.

The downtown express shrieked and clattered through one station after another. Kalman thought about what Zeitman had told Rivkin, about how the dark spark, *botzina d'qardinuta*, and the world that is coming, *alma d'ah-tay*, must not only couple but must also relinquish themselves in order for creation to issue from their union. All this talk about ultimate truth is just a silly intellectual game, a diversion. The self attains its apotheosis not in filling itself with yet another new and titillating insight, but in the moment it surrenders itself to its lover. It is about getting your ego out of the way.

And Moshe de Leon, the author of the Zohar, figured out that *knowing* ultimate truth and *giving* yourself to your lover are effectively identical. You move from this World of Separation to the World of Unity by giving yourself away, and once you can do that, new life is the reward. *Botzina d'qardinuta* and *alma d'ah-tay* were also Moshe de Leon's way of telling this to his lover. Kalman thanked Artie Shaw and removed the little earphone from his ear.

"Of course. How could I have been so dense for so long?" Kalman said. "You can only have it if you give it away!" He whispered it to himself again slowly. "I'll be a sonofabitch! *That's* what it means. . . ."

Kalman rummaged through his bag and removed the Eisenbogen article on *The Book of Love*. He wanted to read the last page again—nothing more than a few lines from a lost book, a fragment of a fragment. This one began with Song of Songs 4:9: "You have stolen my heart with one glance." Its anonymous author then offers the following comment: "This is spoken, as it were, by God to Israel. But it is also spoken by the *botzina d'qardinuta*, a dark spark, to the mother-womb of *alma d'ah-tay*, the world that is coming and from which this world in all its manifold diversity issues and through which we . . ." And right there, in the middle of *that* sentence, the text became illegible, as if it faded back into the ether.

The train rattled, jerked, and finally screeched to a stop.

The doors rolled open and Kalman stepped out onto the platform. He was alone in the bright sunlight. Walking toward him from an alleyway was a goat, a stray nanny goat.

SAFED: SEVENTH ITERATION

The animal stopped, and for a few moments they surveyed each other, the rabbi and the goat, whereupon the goat abruptly turned around and continued walking along the side of the mountain, the rabbi following right behind. (As it says in Midrash Numbers Rabba, "A person is led along whichever path he chooses.") The goat's hooves made a rhythmic clicking sound on the cobblestones. Kalman realized he had quickened his pace in order to keep up with the animal. This is crazy, he thought. I have a perfectly good government-certified guide back at the hotel.

Kalman hesitated as the animal stopped to sniff some trash in the gutter. Whereupon the goat looked up over her shoulder straight at Kalman and bleated. The rabbi was hooked. Two more switchbacks, then a sharp left turn. And . . . the goat was gone. Kalman was standing at the front of the gate to a small synagogue. It was wide open. For a moment, he thought he saw a large red, blue, and white neon sign with a flashing arrow that said: TOWER RECORDS. Or maybe it said: PACKARD. Or perhaps something more obvious, like ENTER HERE. Or, for that matter, CITGO. So Kalman walked inside.

Bright sunlight flooded the room. But other than the light, this time there was Nothing—no chairs, no tables, no ark. No walls, no roof, no floor. A lightlike radiance streaming through windows that were not there on a wall that was not there, overlooking distant mountains that were not there. Only an empty space full of light. A light so bright, it was more like a hardened seed. A spark of darkness. From such a room, anything is possible. "Go ahead," a woman's voice said. "Please, I pray, give it to me. It's mine. Don't you understand? It is addressed to me. Can't you see that? It has *my* name on it. . . ."

Or then again, maybe it was just sunstroke.

That's the thing. These kinds of moments, these kinds of encounters, in addition to their obvious ineffability, transience, and mystery, invariably seem to tolerate two mutually exclusive interpretations: They are the results of entirely explainable natural causes, or they are the results of an incursion of some *other order of being* into this sublunar one. And here's the crazy part: To the one to whom they happen, it doesn't much matter; the revelation is the same either way. Go figure.

MANHATTAN

"Dr. Isabel Benveniste?" said the FedEx deliveryman standing at her office door.

"Yes."

"Letter for you. It requires your signature."

It was snowing outside—only flurries, but enough to cover

the gray ice crust of last week's blizzard with a new coat of white. The city's streets were hopelessly clogged again with holiday traffic. The radiator in Isabel's office hissed uselessly. Despite her Nordic ski sweater, she was still freezing.

The FedEx man handed her an electronic clipboard with an attached stylus and tapped the screen. "Right here, line ten, please."

The return address read, "K. Stern."

The courier closed the door behind him. Isabel pulled the zipper tab across the top of the cardboard envelope. Inside she found a manila folder held closed with rubber bands. Inside the folder were two very thick sheets of cardboard protecting a large Ziploc plastic bag. Inside that was a single, very old piece of paper. It was neatly taped on two corners to a heavy white matte board. "Oh, my God," she gasped, realizing that the letters were Hebrew. "It's Kalman's page, the one he was always talking about! This is that letter from the Livorno Zohar . . . and, yes, here it is, just like he said, that erasure at the top." She looked back inside the folder, and then in the envelope, but there was nothing else, no letter, no note, just the page. "My God," she whispered, "he's gone and given me the most precious thing he has."

She walked over to the window to see it better. "He has turned it back into a love letter."

Even to her untutored eye, it was beautiful, mysterious, sensual. She could not read it, though the writing was disturbingly legible. "Who wrote you?" she said to the page. "And why did you wind up in Kalman's Zohar? And now he has gone and given you . . ." She paused. "And, I think, yes, himself to me."

She fumbled through her purse for her cell phone. In frustration she finally dumped its contents onto her desk.

"Hello, Kalman," she said. "The letter came; the FedEx man just brought it."

"That is good," he said, "because it's got *your* name on it. I mean, I think I'm *supposed* to give it to you. I mean, I believe it has come to me so that I could give it to you."

She did not speak, but he could hear what sounded like the rustle of Kleenex, and then she blew her nose.

"Kalman . . ."

"Yes?"

"I'm sorry. I didn't think you were capable of something like this."

"That's okay. I didn't think I was, either."

"Kalman, I think that I would like to go to Israel—with you—to that little town, Safed, and maybe meet this caretaker you've told me about."

"I would like to do that, too, Isabel. I would like to do that very much." And even though he was as excited and nervous as he had ever been in his entire life, Kalman Stern spoke fluently, without any hesitation whatsoever.

BOSTON

"Stern! Kalman Stern!" His voice sounded like a foghorn. "Where on God's green earth have you been?"

"What?"

"Everybody else is already back at the bus and you're still up here on the roof."

"I'm really sorry, Mr. Smolens. Time must've got away from me."

"You know, Kalman," said the teacher, locking his arm around the boy's neck, "you might just turn out to be a deep thinker someday."

"Thank you, sir." He was silent as they walked toward the big metal door. Then he said, "Mr. Smolens . . ."

"Yes, Kal."

"Do you really think that every question is contained in that spark of light?"

Smolens looked up at the night sky for a moment. "Yes, I do. And every answer also."

As Kalman held open the door for his teacher, off on the horizon they could both see the new red neon triangle of the big Citgo sign over Kenmore Square. Below the red triangle were big blue neon letters.

The letters said: IT'S ALL GOD.

✦ Index of Citations ✦